I0525027

# FIFTEEN EASY TALES AND STRANGE STORIES

# FIFTEEN EASY TALES
# AND
# STRANGE STORIES

*Bryan H. George*

DIADEM BOOKS

All Rights Reserved. Copyright © 2009 Bryan H. George

No part of this book may be reproduced or transmitted in any form or by any means, graphic, electronic, or mechanical, including photocopying, recording, taping or by any information storage or retrieval system, without the permission in writing from the publisher.

Published by Diadem Books

For information, please contact:

Diadem Books
Ocean Surf
CLASHNESSIE
IV27 4JF
Scotland  UK

www.diadembooks.com

This is a work of fiction. Names, characters and incidents are products of the author's imagination. Any resemblance to persons living or dead is entirely coincidental.

ISBN: 978-0-9559852-2-5

Although all characters in this book are entirely fictitious I have never met an uninteresting person in real life. So I dedicate this book to all the people I have met over the years who have made my life so full and worth living.

# *Table of Contents*

## Tales From Life's Tapestry

## Tales From Lower Moss Village

## Tales Out of the Ordinary

# *Tales From Life's Tapestry*

# AUTUMN DAFFODILS

The couple had been standing studying the painting for some time. Both were in their fifties. The man in his casually expensive jacket and trousers had the appearance of a successful retired company executive, and the woman, in her smart tailored costume and immaculate coiffure, the appearance of a businesswoman at the peak of her career.

"Look, Margaret! He hasn't signed it! Perhaps we should!" the man said, taking a felt-tipped pen from his pocket.

"Don't you dare," the woman replied, laughing as she grabbed the pen.

The room attendant who had been watching them approached and tactfully said, "A strange subject 'Autumn Daffodils,' but there is great depth of feeling in the work for such a young artist."

"You know the artist?" the man asked.

"Yes. There are other works of his on display, but they pale beside this one," the attendant replied.

"Yet he hasn't signed it. Did he say why?" the man asked.

"Something very strange. He said it wasn't finished. He had to see how the larger canvas went first."

The three stood in silence for a minute studying the painting before Margaret commented, "An apt title. You have to experience the darkness before you can appreciate the true colour of joy."

The man nodded his agreement and the couple walked away arm in arm exchanging smiles, but as they reached the room exit they stopped and the man called back, "When you see the artist again tell him he can sign it. The larger canvas goes well."

It was nearly two years before that Margaret had first seen the painting. Her granddaughter, Cheryl, had run into the house, her blonde hair tousled and her pink and white cheeks aglow from the cold of an early Autumn morning. "It was horrible, Gran. It had red a sky, blue grass and black trees," she blurted out.

"What had?" Margaret asked.

"The man's painting."

"Lots of people paint our wood. They all see something different," Margaret said gently.

Cheryl's mother called from the kitchen, "This was certainly different, it was angry—intense—frightening in its despair."

Margaret laughed. "It must have been. Was he young and bohemian?"

"No, neither; middle aged, maybe older, difficult to tell under his smock and hat. He looked at me as if he had seen a ghost when I spoke to him," Cheryl's mother replied.

"He was ever so old, like you, Gran, and he had white hair, and a funny pointed beard," Cheryl burst out.

"Cheryl! Gran isn't old," her mother chided.

"And I don't have a funny pointed beard," Margaret said laughing.

Cheryl continued unabashed, "He said he used to paint our wood years ago and that was how he remembered it. You must go and see it, Gran."

"Perhaps tomorrow. I have some work to do now," Margaret replied.

The sun was high in a blue sky the following morning when Margaret walked alone down the lane. She had told herself a hundred times that it couldn't be Patrick after all these years. It was hard to imagine him as anything but a wild young artist with a shock of red hair, and she wasn't sure that she wanted to see him as anything else, yet she had to know for certain if he had come back, and if so, why?

At the path where artists came to paint their interpretations of the pollarded willows two men had set up their easels, and were deep into their work with their backs to her.

Could the older one really be Patrick, acclaimed by every leading art critic in New York? He was too far away for her to be certain. It had been a long time since they had last met. She hesitated, still unsure that she could forgive him, even wanted to forgive him. Then there were his letters. What would his reaction be when, or if, she told him that they had been burnt unread as soon as received?

Quietly she approached the younger man who had set up his easel under a tree. He wore frayed jeans and a paint splattered sweatshirt. His black hair was tied in a rough pigtail. A first year student, she decided.

He turned on his stool. "Realism. Not me," he said.

"But it's very good. Sometimes painting what you are told to paint makes you look with different eyes," Margaret countered.

"You a painter too?" he queried, eyeing her well-cut tweeds. Then his eyes focused on her hands with their narrow palms and long sensitive fingers, and he knew.

"A commercial artist," she replied. His change of expression made her smile, and there was laughter in her hazel eyes as she spoke again. "You don't approve of commercial art. You are young. Pop Art was the vogue in my youth, but Abstract Expressionism was really my scene."

"But why commercial art now?"

"I wasn't wild enough to become famous, and I had to live."

"You must have a good job."

"I have, but money blunts the cutting edge of creativity."

"Money hasn't blunted his," the student said, indicating the older man who had stopped painting, and was staring straight ahead.

In the morning sunshine Margaret could see an auburn tint to the greying hair, and her heart missed a beat. She steadied herself on the tree.

"You alright?" the young man asked.

"Yes, well no, I feel queasy. I must have picked up a virus. I think I had better go home," she said.

At the gate she paused and looked back. The older man had started to paint again, but even at that distance she could see the tension in his body. She hesitated, torn between a rekindled desire and an anger that had smouldered for years, and then she turned and hurried home.

Her daughter was just leaving the house when Margaret arrived.

"Mother! You look terrible," she said.

"I'll be alright if I lie down for a little. I think I've caught something," Margaret replied.

"Caught something," she repeated to herself as she lay back on her bed. "Never lost it would be nearer the truth."

What business had he to come back and open old wounds, she thought. Why come now? She had been divorced for fifteen years and he hadn't even contacted her. It wasn't as if his marriage had been one of abiding love. True, his wife was, had been, breathtakingly beautiful, but she had never tried to hide her infidelity, that was obvious from the press reports on her dalliances. There was a time when he would only have had to snap his fingers and she would have gone running to him, wife or no wife.

Now that his wife was dead he had come back to her, but it was too late; if he were there tomorrow she would tell him so.

That night she slept badly and was awake when dawn broke to a clear sky. She had half hoped it would be raining, then there would have been no point in going to the woods, but the sky was almost cloudless as she walked down the lane.

He was there again, this time alone. Margaret walked across the grass, dappled with sunlight and shadows thrown by the trees. She had discarded her tweeds in favour of a trouser suit, and used just a little more makeup than was her normal custom.

Any doubts that she had that it was Patrick had been dispelled. She stopped behind him and studied his painting of blue grass, red sky, and black branches twisted in agony. He didn't move, and she was sure that he must be able to hear her heart pounding. All the bitter and carefully rehearsed words fled from her mind.

"Why come back here?" she asked, in a hoarse whisper she hardly recognised as her voice.

"I heard that you had returned to your mother's old home."

"That was fifteen years ago. My daughter has it now."

"I had to start somewhere. I had an idea that we might…"

He stopped speaking and continued painting. The voice was older but the magic was still there and Margaret felt the terrible aching, resolutely put behind her so many years ago, come rushing back.

"Might what?" she asked.

Patrick avoided the question and said, "You never replied to my letters."

"Can you blame me?"

"No," he replied and put down his brush.

Margaret stepped back to gain a better appreciation of the incomplete work.

"How you must hate this place," she said.

"I hate what happened here."

"But it was you made it happen."

"Will you never forgive me? I was so young and your sister so seductive," he replied and reached out for her hand.

Almost unaware of what she was doing she stepped forward and took it in hers. The touch of his fingers sent tremors through her body. Anger and resentment welled up again.

"But my sister of all people," she said, and tears filled her eyes. If only she hadn't come along that day years ago she might never have known. A few hours of madness, and three lives ruined. Three? No, not three, for all her contrition, her sister hadn't suffered.

"What did your sister tell you?" Patrick asked.

"She said you seduced her. I believed her, for nearly ten years I believed her, until my husband told me the truth shortly before he left me. He laughed at me. He told me of all the men she had seduced, including him."

There was a long silence before Patrick slowly raised his gaze to meet hers.

"Are you happy?" he asked.

"I have a daughter and a granddaughter that I love, a good job, and my art."

"And yet you came back," he said.

"Were you happy?" Margaret countered, but she already knew the answer.

For what seemed an eternity neither of them spoke and only the rustle of the breeze in the leaves broke the silence. Then Margaret picked up a paintbrush. Thoughtfully she mixed some yellow paint. This time she must make the right decision. Patrick watched without seeing, savouring her presence. Slowly she began to put the yellow onto his canvas.

Neither of them was aware of the student's arrival until a shocked young voice behind them said, "What are you doing?"

Margaret finished painting, then turned to the student and replied, "Putting in daffodils."

"Daffodils in Autumn?" the student asked with a nervous laugh.

"Sometimes Spring comes a little late in life," Margaret replied.

Patrick took the painting off the easel, handed it to the student, and said, "It's yours. Finish it. I have a larger canvas that will demand my undivided attention."

# THE HANDKERCHIEF

Single again, Jason felt depressed and acutely conscious of the anonymity of a London Street as he walked with a purposeful air while trying to decide where to have his snack lunch. With a well-groomed head of hair showing an auburn tint, slightly overweight and conventionally dressed for a senior partner in a small firm of accountants he was inconspicuous in the bustling city crowd. His personal assistant had once described him as a man with stifled potential.

On an impulse, unusual for him, he pushed open the door of a wine-bar he had passed many times on his way to have lunch at a rather expensive French restaurant with his now ex-wife.

The wine bar was crowded but there was no way he could fail to notice the woman at a window table. She was the centre figure of a small group, in her forties, large, loud and obviously successful. Her coiffeur was immaculate and she was dressed in the latest designer clothes. As Jason approached the bar he heard her blow her nose like a foghorn.

In response to Jason's raised eyebrows the bartender was only too pleased to tell him that she ran a string of boutiques in the city and was a lunchtime regular with a standing order of smoked salmon sandwiches for ten and two bottles of Chablis.

"Ten?" Jason queried counting the small group.

"Sure, but two got the boot a few weeks back. Got drunk at a reception and let out something about her winter range to a competitor."

A group of city types called for champagne and the bartender left to serve them.

The woman was in full flow. She had been at Ascot as a hospitality guest of one of her major suppliers. Jason recognised the brand name

6

as one he had seen on his ex-wife's last purchase before she left him. He could hardly forget that outfit. When he received his credit card account he thought she had bought a diamond ring.

"Never seen money change hands so fast," the woman boomed.

"There's big money in racing," one of her entourage ventured.

"Straight into the bookies' pockets. Quickest money making system ever invented. Should have thought of it before I got caught up in fashion."

"So you didn't have a flutter?" another voice queried.

"Good God no, man, but I enjoyed the hats."

The bartender returned from serving the champagne. "What's her name?" Jason asked.

"Harriet."

"A diminutive of Henrietta I suppose. She doesn't sound like a Henrietta," Jason observed.

"She'll sound even less like it if you ever call her that!"

Jason laughed. He could well believe it. The verve and enthusiasm of the woman had grabbed him. She was beautiful in a majestic way.

"I wonder if she needs an accountant," he mused.

It was a rhetorical question, but the bartender took it as addressed to him and asked, "You an accountant then?"

"Yes. A senior partner."

"One of the big five, or is it three now?"

"No, a medium sized partnership."

"Then you're in with a chance; she's had it up to here with the big boys and I'd say you're fit and under fifty. Her husband did the accounts until she traced some entertaining expenses back to a weekend with a model from the agency. He's now her ex and the business hasn't looked back since."

"How do you know she's had it up to here with the big boys?" Jason asked ignoring, but not missing, the point about his age.

"The whole bar knows when she's annoyed, but don't try your luck here; she may moan in mega decibels but she won't do business in a bar."

At that moment Harriet's voice boomed out again: "He had the nerve to say we could discuss it over lunch. So I said I cancel orders over lunch and the bigger the lunch the more I cancel. That shut him up!"

"And got you into the enclosure at Ascot," a follower added.

Harried gave a roar of laughter and the bartender said, "See what I mean?"

"Are they business associates?" Jason asked.

"Oh yes they are, most of them anyway. It pays to be in the cabal but you don't last long there if you spoil her lunch!"

Jason left the bar in a reflective mood. He was badly in need of a rich successful client but he wondered if someone accustomed to dealing with the likes of KPMG or Price Waterhouse, would put her financial affairs in his hands. Of course they wouldn't, he told himself, she might have had it up to the neck with them but that didn't mean she would want anything less; yet that didn't stop him from wondering if there might be a chance.

After that first visit he became a regular in the wine bar for his snack lunch when working from the office but an opportunity to meet the imposing Harriet never presented itself until one Friday afternoon, some weeks after his first visit. She was in a hurry and had finished earlier than usual but before she rose to go she produced a box of new handkerchiefs, man size. "Collected them from Harrods today," she boomed.

"Monogrammed as usual?" a member of her entourage asked.

"Naturally! Hand-sewn! See!" she said, pulling one out and waving it in the enquirer's face before blowing into it with a mighty blast.

Jason resisted the temptation to applaud and watched in admiration as she left the building like a galleon in full sail. It was only after she and her entourage had gone that he saw a second handkerchief had come out of the box and fallen to the floor.

The bar tender was occupied with a complex order at that moment and Jason took the opportunity to pick up the handkerchief en route to the toilet and slip it into his briefcase. All he had to do now was to find an opportune moment to return it and work out some way of letting her know he was an accountant. He thought no one had noticed his actions but he had underestimated the ability of an experienced bartender to miss nothing of importance that went on in his bar.

On the following Monday Jason had an appointment at the Manchester office of a London client and would not be returning until the early train on Wednesday. He always travelled north by train; he found it relaxing and it gave him an opportunity to gather his thoughts together on the job ahead, but on this occasion they became focussed on what he was going to say when he returned the handkerchief. It would be only too easy for the opportunity to become a mere polite gesture followed by a brief word of appreciation and it had to be on the Wednesday; any later than that the new handkerchiefs would have become stale news.

By the time he reached his hotel he had decided on his course of action. He would choose his moment carefully before she started her meal and approach her, handkerchief in hand, saying, "I think you dropped this rather fine piece of embroidery the other day, beautiful needlework. I once had a client who manufactured machine sewn labels, but this is surely hand stitched."

Pleased with the idea, he left the hotel and took a taxi to his client's office where he stayed until midday. After declining an invitation to lunch on principle he set off on foot to an Italian restaurant which had tables for two set along wall seats, far enough apart to give a sense of privacy and close enough to be friendly.

It was a short walk that took him through a busy shopping centre and on his arrival he found the restaurant equally busy. The head waiter recognised him, showed him to an unoccupied wall table next to one with a couple of young executive types deep in conversation across their table. They didn't even look up as Jason sat down on the wall seat.

After ordering the "Chef's special fish soup", lasagne and a glass of house wine, Jason opened 'The Times' he had bought at Euston Station and started to glance through it, but as he turned the pages, he became aware of a couple sitting at a table in the centre of the room. The woman looked to be in her early thirties and from her sallow skin and jet-black hair Jason decided she was probably South American. She was wearing a black jacket, black skirt and white blouse with crimson embroidery. The man was about the same age as his companion, casually smart, slim, blond and handsome in a Teutonic way; Jason could see that he would go down well with women. They were deep in conversation but every now and then she would glance across the room and her face would light up with a dazzling smile of white teeth against blood red lips. It was on one of those occasions that she caught Jason's eye and for a moment he received the full benefit of her charm before she continued her conversation with her companion.

Although he occasionally glanced in her direction after that he was not granted a second dazzling smile but he had the feeling that the woman was watching him.

He returned to the restaurant on the following day and felt a sense of disappointment as he looked around and saw that the woman with the smile was not there. The waiter took him to a wall table, handed him the menu and hesitated to see if he would be ordering immediately. It was at that moment that the couple arrived, glanced round the restaurant and then walked straight to the waiter.

"This table, is it taken?" the man asked and pointed to the table next to Jason's. The waiter appeared a little surprised but assured them it was not taken. It didn't occur to Jason till much later that their selection of the table next to his was more than a coincidence.

"Good afternoon, my name is Klaus and this is Carmen, we are touring your beautiful country," the man said as soon as they had ordered their meal.

"I'm Jason. Here on business. Pleased to meet you," Jason replied.

"On business; that is a pity, but perhaps you tell us where to go. Would you suggest the Lakes?"

"Yes, you must visit the Lake District, if you have time," Jason replied.

"I think I would first like to see the place you call Trafford Centre in Manchester, ees it like Oxford Street?" Carmen asked, her thin silk blouse displaying her cleavage to its full advantage as she leant forward across the table. Jason felt a premonition of disaster. That was nothing new for him. It was usually stimulated by immoral thoughts, as his ex-wife had pointed out more than once, but on this occasion the sensation was of an intensity he had not experienced for a long time.

Klaus gave Carmen a disapproving look and said, "You always spend the money."

Jason laughed. "It's nothing like Oxford Street, but you can certainly spend the money there."

"Shopping, shopping! Women! They can think of nothing else! I hope it is not too expensive. The cost of shopping in London makes me, how do you put it? Faint?" Klaus said, and forced a laugh.

"I hope you saw more than Oxford Street when you were in London," Jason said and that set Klaus off on a rundown on all the places they had visited and what they thought of them; so detailed that Jason suspected that he was often quoting from a guidebook. He had just finished describing their visit to The Tate when Jason's soup arrived, a different chef's special to that of the previous day.

Jason folded The Times he had bought in the local shopping area at the crossword and concentrated on that and his soup which was followed by a dish of spaghetti bolognaise, but the couple on the next table intrigued him and he couldn't help hearing snatches of their conversation. They were speaking in Spanish, a language in which he was reasonably fluent but in dialect he found difficulty in following. He gathered that Klaus was expounding on the state of European politics, a subject which appeared to be close to his heart but obviously bored Carmen who gave noncommittal answers, and let a little smile twitch at the corner of her lips when she succeeded in catching Jason's eye. Slightly disconcerted, Jason finished his meal quickly, ordered a cup of coffee and opened his paper so that he couldn't see the tantalising Carmen.

He had just finished reading the leader when Carmen's raised voice alerted him to the quarrel that was taking place across the next table. Klaus sounded icily cool and in complete control of his emotions but not so Carmen who suddenly came out with a torrent of invective.

Jason turned to the obituaries and tried to ignore what was happening but the quarrel didn't abate and out of the corner of his eye he could see the waiter, a few tables away, looking concerned. Suddenly, just as the waiter started to walk in the direction of the quarrelling couple, Klaus stood up, slammed some money down on the table and stalked out of the restaurant.

Carmen burst into a flood of tears.

Jason was at a loss what to do. He felt drawn to comfort this young woman with the mouth that twitched so invitingly, yet he didn't want to become involved. He lowered his paper and ventured a glance in her direction. She was alternately mopping up her tears and blowing her nose, but she managed a little girl in distress glance at him over her handkerchief. The premonition of disaster came surging back. He looked to the waiter who just shrugged noncommittally and returned to the diners he had been serving before the outburst.

Carmen's sobs gradually became less and less as she continued to dab her eyes and Jason was wondering if, having been introduced earlier, he should make some comment when she dropped her now sodden handkerchief on the table and started to rummage in her handbag for another, but without success.

He put down his paper and made a show of feeling in his pockets for a clean one but only succeeded in pulling out one he had obviously used. Then he remembered Harriet's embroidered linen specimen that was still in his briefcase. That, he decided, would be too great a sacrifice; anyway, this was a domestic matter and he would be best off keeping out of it. He picked up his paper again and returned to reading the obituaries.

He had barely finished a two-column contribution about a worthy benefactor whom he had never heard of when he caught a strong odour of perfume and felt Carmen's hand rest lightly on his. For a moment he thought she was standing beside him but, as he lowered his paper, he saw that she had moved to the chair across the table from him.

"I am veree sorree; Klaus, he can bee a peeg!" she sniffed and the tears started to flow again. She grabbed Jason's napkin and started mopping her face with it. Too late Jason noticed it had suffered from being put down on the remains of his meal and streaks of bolognaise sauce joined the tears and mascara. By now the diners nearby had stopped eating, and were watching, fascinated.

Carmen gripped Jason's hand. Drastic action was called for. With difficulty he released her hold, opened his briefcase and with a flourish worthy of the sacrifice he was making, brought out 'The Handkerchief from Harrods'.

"Please accept this," he said.

With a sinking feeling he watched it gradually discolour as it mopped up a mixture of tears, bolognaise and makeup. Finally she popped it into her handbag, took both Jason's hands and said, "How can I thank you?"

Jason hastily withdrew his hands. "It was the least I could do," he replied.

At that moment the waiter appeared and put a plate down on the table. "Your bill, madam," he said coldly.

Carmen retrieved the money that Klaus had left on their table and put it on the plate.

"That will only pay for one," the waiter said.

Carmen gave a gasp, looked at the bill and then studied what she had put on the plate.

"Klaus, he give me five pound notes, not tens—he ees impossible," she said, took a wallet from her handbag and shook the contents onto the table; a few silver coins fell out. She returned to her handbag but failed to produce any further cash.

"Perhaps madam could pay by credit card," the Waiter said.

"No! Klaus, he has my credit cards. He says I spend too much with the credit cards," she whispered and wiped her right eye with the back of her hand to remove a tear.

The Waiter showed no sympathy and said, "Then the gentleman will have to pay."

"Steady on!" Jason retorted.

"Not you, sir. The one who came in with her."

"Oh no, Klaus he will kill me. He doesn't know I spend all the monee I get from the bank in your London," Carmen howled.

"That is not my problem madam. I am afraid you will have to stay here until he returns to settle the bill," the waiter said.

"But what if he does not return?" Carmen asked and Jason thought she was going to start crying again but she appeared to have run out of tears.

"Then it will be a matter for the police," the waiter replied.

Carmen gasped and looked pathetically at the waiter whose expression didn't change, he had seen it all before, so she directed her dark soulful eyes in Jason's direction.

Wondering if he was being conned, and knowing that the waiter was sure of it, he picked up the money that Klaus had given Carmen, handed over his credit card and said, "Put the two bills together. I'll find the gentleman."

As the waiter left them Carmen grasped both of Jason's hands and purred, "Oh! Why can't my Klaus be like you? I go now and mend my makeup. Then I find him. He will be angry with me but eet will pass."

Before Jason could make any comment she was gone.

Fifteen minutes later she hadn't returned and any doubt that Jason might have had that he was the victim of a confidence trick was replaced by the certain knowledge that he was, yet it seemed very elaborate for the amount of money involved and he sat for another ten minutes finishing the dregs of his coffee waiting for the next move. Eventually the knowing glances of the waiter and whispered remarks of the other diners became too much for him; he carefully folded his paper, stood up and left, making as dignified an exit as he could.

He stopped outside the restaurant for a moment and looked up and down the road hoping, but not expecting to see, Carmen and Klaus. There was no sign of them and he set off walking back to the office. He was in the shopping centre weaving his way through a mêlée of mums with toddlers and businessmen and women returning to work when someone grabbed his arm from behind. He spun round to see it was Carmen with her makeup fully restored. Before he could say anything she shouted, "It ees my hero," and flung her arms round his neck, kissed him full on the mouth and then stepped back. He just had time to see Klaus approaching, before she repeated the performance.

A few heads turned and gave them amused smiles before Klaus arrived and dragged her off the bemused Jason.

"Slut," he said and slapped her across the face.

That was too much for Jason. He pushed Klaus aside and stepped between them; for a few seconds he and Klaus glared at one another and before Jason had collected his wits, Klaus shouted, "Bastard! You seduce my wife!" and pushed Jason so roughly that he stumbled back, then stepped forward, his face contorted in anger and his arms raised as if he was going to grab Jason by the neck.

In his twenties Jason had played rugby at county level and still kept himself fit but the punch he landed on Klaus's chin surprised him. The man's knees buckled and he collapsed onto the concrete floor. Carmen screamed and dropped onto her knees beside Klaus's prostrate body. She looked up at Jason and stared at Klaus's prostrate body and then at Jason. Her eyes were no longer soft and appealing but blazing with anger as she shouted, "You keell him, you keell my Klaus!"

Jason bent over the prostrate body and felt his pulse. "He's not dead," he assured her but she wouldn't listen and continued shouting, "He keell my Klaus, he keell my husband!"

Jason stood up and took a couple of steps back as someone announcing they were a paramedic knelt down. A crowd had gathered and Jason was beginning to feel distinctly uncomfortable when Klaus suddenly sat bolt upright and was grabbed in an embrace by Carmen. A murmur ran through the crowd and people began to drift away.

It occurred to Jason that no one seemed very interested in him and probably the few people who actually saw him hit Klaus had slipped away so as not to become involved. It seemed a good time to follow their example.

It was on the TV regional news which Jason was watching in the hotel lounge where he saw a glamorous picture of Carmen and heard the report of an assault in the local shopping centre. The announcer said, 'This morning a portly middle-aged man made advances to a South American beauty and then knocked her husband unconscious …'

"Portly gentleman! Barely a kilo overweight!" Jason snorted.

The other occupants of the lounge looked round so he did the same. The announcer went on to tell of an unprovoked and brutal attack on a wronged husband that bore as little resemblance to what had occurred as did the description of him. He was beginning to feel he had very little to worry about until, at the end of the brief report, the announcer said, "A spokesperson for the police said that CCTV footage of cameras in the shopping centre were being examined but there should be no trouble in tracing the assailant from a monogrammed handkerchief that he lent to the woman."

When he returned to London and his office next morning he found an urgent request for assistance from a long-standing client on the other side of London. It appeared that their main customer had gone into receivership and, despite many warnings from Jason, they had relied too heavily on that customer's business; now they were facing the possibility that they too might be dragged into insolvency.

Jason wasted no time in going to his client; it would give him a chance to collect his thoughts in case the police contacted him. They were bound to trace the owner of the handkerchief quite quickly, and while he was almost sure no one had seen him pick it up, and Harriet probably had no idea where she had dropped it, he couldn't be certain.

He was right regarding the time the police took to trace the owner of the handkerchief but wrong on the second point; the bartender lost no time in telling Harriet where she had lost her handkerchief and who had picked it up.

Jason's client's situation was as bad as he had feared and it took up most of the week and two days into the following week before he was able to return to a normal routine. During that time he had his daily lunch snack with his client on the other side of London which meant he could put off deciding whether or not to continue visiting the wine bar and find out if Harriet had heard from the police.

It was on the Wednesday, two weeks after the episode in the shopping centre, as he was walking from his office towards the wine bar and still trying to decide if he should go in, that a car drew up on the other side of the road and Harriet's voice boomed: "Jason I want a word!"

He stopped and his heart missed a beat; so they knew—she had noticed him in the bar!

"Jason!" the voice boomed again, "See you in the pub."

He hesitated, then waved in acknowledgement, but his pace grew slower as he approached his destination. He felt sure Harriet wouldn't call the police—that wasn't her style—but this was not the sort of introduction that he had been planning. As he hesitated at the door someone pushed past him, opening it wide—and there she was at her usual table surrounded by her entourage.

"Come and join us. Thought you had emigrated!" she boomed.

He stepped into the bar and glanced at the bartender who gave him an encouraging wink; then he walked across to Harriet's table with a show of confidence that he didn't feel.

"This is the man who flattened our Klaus," Harriet boomed, introducing Jason to her entourage.

"You know Klaus?" he asked, amazed.

"Know him! Know the *pair* of them. Took my shops for thousands. Couldn't believe they didn't realise whose handkerchief they had. Just shows how important attention to detail can be!"

"So where are they now?"

"Who knows? Not in England, that's for sure after what I gave to the police. They were just too quick. Slippery as eels. Pity you didn't do a proper job and put him in hospital. Still, can't blame you. You weren't to know! One thing for sure, they won't be suing you now they know the owner of the handkerchief. The police gave the handkerchief back to me. Wondered if you might like it as a souvenir?" she boomed so all the bar could hear and poured Jason a glass of Chablis.

"Plenty more where that came from," she said as he sipped it appreciatively. "Believe you're an accountant? Never met one with a good right hook before. Come to my office nine sharp tomorrow and we'll talk business."

# THREE WEEKS IN BOGNOR REGIS

Clair slammed the back door behind her, took a half empty bottle of wine out of the fridge and poured herself a glass. Her chic appearance belied an exhausting day in her boutique with one assistant on maternity leave.

She sat down at the Formica topped table, looked round the kitchen, and thought; really, a new kitchen and three weeks in Bognor Regis would have made more sense than this super cruise. Peter and I would still be able to eat out at Lugi's on Friday evenings like we used to.

It had been a state of the art kitchen fifty years ago. It still looked pretty good in an old fashioned way, but Claire and Peter had been saving to have a completely new one installed to celebrate their twenty-fifth wedding anniversary, that is, until Peter suggested, "Let's use the money for a super, once in a lifetime, cruise instead."

It had seemed a great idea at the time; their son had a flat and a job fifty miles away in Bradford and their daughter was in residence at Manchester University. They could start saving again for the kitchen as soon as they returned. So, in a moment of euphoria, they had booked and paid the deposit on what the travel agent had described as 'A Dream Cruise to the Far East'.

It didn't take them long to realise that there were hidden expenses in going on a dream cruise and there was also the problem of Sarah, Claire's widowed mother who lived alone in a mews flat conversion quarter of a mile away. She was quite capable of looking after herself but ever since she turned seventy almost a year ago Peter had become obsessed with the idea that the neighbours considered Sarah's welfare to be his responsibility and he insisted that they must find someone to stay in the flat while they were on the cruise.

Well, they hadn't. Both their children were living miles away, and all the rest of the family had equally good reasons for being unavailable.

In one of her depressed moments Claire had said to Peter, "Perhaps we should forfeit our deposit and go to Bognor Regis; we had a great time there on our honeymoon."

"Never!" Peter had replied. "If all else fails it'll have to be three weeks in a residential home for your mother. I can arrange an increased overdraft facility; I might as well take advantage of being a bank manager and we've plenty of collateral. I'll look around but don't say anything until I've found somewhere, and swear the kids to secrecy."

Claire shuddered at the thought of her mother in a residential home. For one thing, Sarah was not residential home friendly. She was tall, slim, active and a great organiser like her daughter, but there the similarity ended. Claire, as her mother put it, was a walking boutique while Sarah was seldom seen in anything but sensible trousers and a sweater which would have been as much out of place in a residential home as her robust outlook on life.

Claire finished her glass of wine, took four lamb chops out of the fridge and was searching for a package of mixed vegetables in the freezer when Peter arrived home. She noticed immediately that he had removed his tie, a sure sign that he hadn't come straight from the bank.

"I've done it!" he announced.

She gave him a welcoming kiss and said, "When we've changed you can tell me what you've been up to while I do the chops and you see to the veg." But he wasn't listening.

"I've found a decent Residential Home at a price we can just about afford."

"Already? Mother won't go!"

"She'll have to go. We're not cancelling the cruise and there's no way I'll leave her alone in the flat. She might have a fall or something and then what would the neighbours think?"

"All you ever worry about is what the neighbours think. The neighbours would be only too pleased to keep an eye on her. They do so already. If it hadn't been for them she'd have swapped her 'Punto' for that second-hand 'Mini Cooper' on her seventieth without telling us!"

"Interfering busybodies," a voice said from the kitchen door.

Claire turned round and gasped. "Mother! What are you doing here at this time of day?"

"I've come to give you my news. You've been arguing. It's about what to do with me while you're on that cruise I'm not supposed to know about, I suppose. Your daughter let it slip out weeks ago. Of course you don't want an old battleaxe tagging along, spoiling your second honeymoon."

"No one called you an old battleaxe, and it's not a second honeymoon, it's our twenty-fifth wedding anniversary celebration," Peter retorted.

"You have a point. You're hardly honeymoon material now. Anyway, I would be perfectly safe in my flat, if that were the only option."

Peter strode to the window and said grimly, "It's not the only option and there is no way you're going to stay there alone. If you had an accident…"

"What would the neighbours say?" Clare's mother finished for him.

"Stop it, you two. You'll spoil everything," Claire shouted.

"I suppose you know about the Home too?" Peter said, ignoring Claire.

"No, but if you've made a reservation you can cancel it!"

Claire intervened, "Mother, it's only for three weeks and you would be with people of your own generation."

"Bah! Stop being ageist. What's your next suggestion? That I stay with my grandson and his girlfriend? Is that why he's been so quiet recently? I'm not surprised. I'd probably interrupt them in a passionate embrace, having it off on the hearthrug."

"Mother!"

Peter turned bright red and slammed his fist on the pine wood dresser rattling the crockery. "We're going, and you're not going to stop us," he shouted.

Claire looked from one to the other in despair.

"Of course you're going," her mother said.

"So you've found a residential home you like," Peter said, his voice heavy with sarcasm.

"No way! I'm going on holiday too."

"A Saga holiday, why didn't we think of it!" Clare laughed with relief.

"Not Saga! Three weeks by the sea with Charlie Thompson."

"Charlie Thomson! Who's he?" Peter gasped.

"Someone I met two years ago, when I was rescuing my sister from that terrible Residential Home in Sussex. He was rescuing his mother at the same time."

"So he doesn't live locally," Peter said with obvious relief.

"No! But he visits me once a month and we go line dancing."

"Is he married?" Peter asked.

"A widower; if things work out while you're away I'll probably move in with him. He has a lovely home in Southport."

"You'll do *what!* How old is he?" Peter gasped.

"Sixty two."

"Only sixty two!"

"Yes, sixty two, retired and very comfortably off."

"So you're planning to stay at his home in Southport while we're away," Claire said.

"No! We'll be on holiday too, staying in the best hotel in Bognor Regis. You've always said it was a great place for a honeymoon."

# ALL IN THE GENES

Jean dumped Frank's overnight bag on the duvet and said, "She might have told you she was dying. If you hadn't decided to arrange to see her while you were down her way she'd have been dead and buried before you knew anything."

Frank zipped up his jeans and pulled on a designer roll-top sweater before answering. "She probably didn't think it was worth mentioning. You know what an independent sod Aunt Emily can be, but I bet our smarmy Cousin Denis has known all along." It was no secret that Denis's mother openly encouraged her son to act as a surrogate son to his great aunt.

Jean refrained from commenting. After all, it was Frank's family, and Aunt Emily had experienced more than her fair share of tragedy. Her first husband, a successful American businessman, had been killed along with their son while flying his private plane, and her second husband had become an alcoholic and died in a car accident. She had never been able to have another child and lived alone in a large five-bedroom country house in Kent.

Spurred on by his wife's obvious disapproval of his jeans and sweater, Frank opened the door of their large built-in wardrobe and took out his only suit, then put it back and rummaged through his assortment of old and new jackets; finally he shut the door again and said, "What's the point? If she hasn't cut me out of her will she'll wonder why I'm all dressed up, and if she has it won't make her change her mind. Anyway, nobody wears a suit these days, not even at fifty—except Cousin Denis, that is."

Jean smiled wryly. Frank's aunt had expressed her disapproval of her nephew's choice of a wife on more than one occasion. "You're right," she said, "she's probably cut you out because of me and saw no point in telling us. Anyway, that outfit should make sure she does if she hasn't. I expect Denis turns up looking like he's come straight from his office in the city. Do you think he chose the Nursing Home? It sounds very exclusive."

Frank laughed. "Definitely not if he's paying, and the same goes if she is. He's probably the main beneficiary in her will and he wouldn't want to see his legacy being spent. Perhaps I should be taking our children to see her. She might have forgotten overhearing our son and heir saying she looked like a witch from Hogwarts Castle and be moved to leaving them something."

The drive from the Midlands to Kent was not one Frank enjoyed and he was in no frame of mind for a meeting with his cousin on arriving. But there was Denis in the leather upholstered atmosphere of the nursing home's lobby that made a perfect backdrop for his immaculate city suit and over the top tie.

He peeled himself off the armchair in which he had been stretched out reading the Financial Times, languidly offered a hand, and said, "So you've got here at last. Wow, those jeans sure say something!"

"You might have told me our aunt was dying," Frank retorted, ignoring the limp hand.

"I like the 'our aunt'. You should keep in touch with our relatives like I do," Denis replied.

"You mean keep in touch with the rich ones. Jean's given up sending you and your lot Christmas cards," Frank retorted

"No need to be like that. But for me the old girl would be in a Council home. Her money's all tied up. Can't get at any of it. Lives off some sort of annuity. But I expect, as the chief executor of her will, I can sort things out when she dies." Denis made to leave.

Frank stepped sideways to stop him and asked, "Who's paying for all this then? Don't tell me you lent her a few quid."

Denis shrugged, "A bit more than a few quid. In fact I settle all the bills. I've had to sell a few shares to do it. Still, she can't last much longer. You're probably only just in time, not that it'll do you and Jean much good."

Frank experienced the uneasy feeling that he always had when talking to Denis. Years of dealing with his father's family had disillusioned him of any ideas he might have had of them being capable of altruism.

"What do you mean, all the bills?" he replied.

"As I just said; it was that or a Council home. Her money's all tied up."

"And what do you get out of it?"

"If you must know, she changed her will; but you were never in it anyway. I get everything after a small legacy to each of her nieces. Should cover the costs with a bit to spare for my trouble."

"You conniving bastard," Frank snapped.

"I think you've got that wrong. You're the bastard in the family," Denis retorted, and tried to push past Frank.

"Now we're being childish," Frank said and pushed back. Caught off balance, Denis stumbled into an armchair.

The receptionist reached under her desk for the alarm bell. Trouble between relatives was not a new experience for her.

Denis sneered from the safety of the chair. "Hasn't anyone told you who your real father was? You'd better ask Aunt Emily, she knows—different genes, is how my mother puts it."

The receptionist's finger found the button but before she could press it an authoritative voice said, "Mr. Frank King, I presume."

Frank turned to see Matron by the reception desk staring at him with obvious disapproval.

"Yes, I've come to see my Aunt."

"I should ask you to leave but as you have come this far you may spend a few minutes with her. Nurse! Take Mr. King to see his Aunt."

A nurse came into the lobby and, in the slightly antiseptic atmosphere of a nursing home, Frank followed her silently down a long heavily carpeted corridor with prints of local beauty spots hung at intervals on both sides. They stopped at the end room on the left and the nurse knocked. A weak voice called, "Come in."

Aunt Emily was lying back in bed wearing a royal blue bed jacket hand embroidered with red flowers that set off her immaculate silver-white hair and pale skin taught over her high cheekbones. Her eyes were closed and she was breathing heavily. Frank thought she looked regal.

"I'll leave you now. If you need me there's a bell push by the bed. Don't make her too exhausted," the nurse said and a smile flickered at the corners of her mouth as she spoke.

Frank wanted to ask her what was so amusing but there was no way he could do so without his aunt hearing.

"Right, thank you," he replied.

As the door closed, Emily sat bolt upright. "So you've come at last!" she said.

'No one told us you were ill. You should have phoned. I would have come immediately," Frank replied.

"Didn't want to bother you. Denis lives much closer. He's been most useful."

"So he told me."

"By your expression I guess you met him on his way out and had an argument. Did he tell you that he's paying the bills?"

"Yes."

"Don't you dare offer to help. I trust you didn't hit him—the nurse hoped you would. I'm very comfortable here and wouldn't want the dragon to throw me out because my nephews came to blows. I expect you met Matron in the lobby."

"I did. She appeared just in time," Frank replied and ran his gaze round the room which was more of a luxurious bed-sit than a bedroom; quality carpet, two easy chairs, small mahogany dining table with two chairs to match and a television set; also a bedside table, wardrobe and chest of drawers, all in mahogany. He assumed that a second door indicated that the accommodation was en suit.

"I expect Denis has told you that I have left my estate to him, apart from a few smallish legacies to my nieces, as compensation for the expense he is incurring. And you think that's a pretty good bargain for him!"

"Something like that. The house alone must be worth a cool million at least!"

"Jealous?—are you?"

"No, I wouldn't change places with Denis at any price. I have a lovely wife, two lovely children and a well paid job that I enjoy."

Emily nodded. "Yes, that dizzy slip of a girl you married has turned out better than you deserved. So I was wrong. I can't always be right."

At that point Matron bustled in, puffed up the pillows and said, "You mustn't tire her. She has had enough excitement for one day. Mr. Denis exhausts her with all his talk about stocks and shares."

Emily glared at Matron. "Excitement be damned. You don't think I listen to him. He only comes to see if I'm dying. Now leave us alone.

We have private business to discuss."

Matron gave a sniff and left.

"I'm not the flavour of the month," Frank said.

"Yes, she obviously doesn't approve of you. Her Mr. Denis; Mr. Denis indeed, who does she think he is. She always brings him in personally and I give them an Oscar performance. What happened in the lobby?"

"We had a few words and I pushed him into a chair."

Emily laughed then spoke more quietly, "Keep your voice down, she's probably listening at the door. The nurses will be sorry you didn't clout him. What upset you? You say you're not jealous."

Frank didn't answer immediately. A moment when he was a child flashed back from deep in his memory; he recalled Denis's mother saying to his mother that he was the spitting image of his father and his mother bursting into tears and rushing out of the room.

Eventually Frank replied, "He said I was a bastard, and I'm sure he meant it literally".

Emily lay back on the pillow with a sigh. "So your mother never told you. There wasn't a right moment I suppose. It's one of those secrets that one doesn't talk about, but it's true. When it happened we were living in America. Our father, your grandfather on your mother's side, was Vice President of an American investment company; he liked the life over there and had the idea of emigrating but mother was dead set against it and eventually he returned to England to set up a British Office. Your real father was an American bomber pilot killed in action in Vietnam. Your mother was pregnant with you when she married my brother."

"If that's true why isn't my real father's name on my birth certificate? Didn't my father realise?"

Aunt Emily laughed. "The answer is greed. It's in our family's genes. Haven't you noticed? Your mother was a real American beauty but more important was that she came with a very good dowry and your father, or should I say stepfather, had courted her unsuccessfully for some time. He had even hinted more than once at a relationship.

"No one in the family, apart from me, being a close friend of your mother, believed you weren't his child and my father insisted he did the right thing by her. I think your stepfather guessed that he wasn't your biological father, but he was, 'hoist on his own petard', as the saying goes. I can still see his face at the christening when people said you looked just like him. It was not until some years later that my sister, Denis's mother, became suspicious."

"That was a bit mean of mother," Denis said.

"Not really. It wasn't acceptable in our social circle to have an illegitimate child in those days and the dowry gave your stepfather a good start in business, particularly, to put it politely, after he renegotiated the figure; and a beautiful wife was a definite asset."

"So you have decided that this entitles Denis to the bulk of your estate when you go," Frank said, more as a statement than a question.

"Of course it does. He's the only male blood relative I have left; and he certainly deserves what he's getting. But to come back to you, your mother wasn't the only person to lose their lover in that raid. The navigator was wickedly handsome too."

Emily stopped for a moment and her expression softened. Then she pulled herself together and continued, "It was wartime. Don't blame your mother. She was in love and one never knew what tomorrow would bring. When she asked me to be your Godmother I couldn't refuse. She thought I would be as devastated as she was but I wasn't pregnant and I was a few years younger than her. I'm not sure I knew what true love was until my son died. Now my flashy nephew Denis thinks he can step into his shoes. Yes, he deserves everything that's coming to him."

"That sounds more like a threat," Frank said, looking uncomprehendingly at his Aunt.

Emily sat bolt upright in bed and said, "Everyone talks about the fortune my first husband made. What they forget is that my second husband was a gambler and latterly an alcoholic. The house is heavily mortgaged and now they've built the motorway almost in the back garden it nearly qualifies as negative equity. Any personal capital I had was swallowed paying off my husband's debts after he was killed."

"But you live very well," Frank protested.

"Yes, I live well, on a large pension I receive from a scheme I took out when I was a director in my first husband's businesses, but it wouldn't run to paying for this nursing home on top of mortgage payments and the like; hence my deal with Denis."

"That he inherits virtually all of your estate provided he pays for the nursing home."

"Got it first time; but don't worry, I took out an endowment policy for you at the same time as I set up my pension. That's my Godson's legacy."

"So how much will Denis get when, when…??

"When I die, no need to be tactful. A well deserved lesson in manipulation and, with a bit of luck and skilful negotiation, more than enough to cover the cost of keeping me here plus at least a hundred thousand. Not, I'm afraid, the million he expects; and don't look so shocked we work that way, it's all in the genes."

# GETTING THE GATES BACK

G BH! He should have killed the guy; if he had he would still be in prison and far better off, Dave thought as he plodded along the suburban street. The many layers of scruffy garments he wore were secured at the waist by a couple of lengths of binder twine and his few worldly possessions were in a sack slung over his shoulder.

He tried not to remember the days when he had lived in a house like one of the terraced dwellings he was passing. Those days had been lost forever and he had long ago given up the thought of trying to rebuild his life.

Soon the appearance of graffiti told him he had left the town's better-off outer suburbs. Now there were large houses that had been turned into cheap flats. As he passed an impressive Church, erected during Queen Victoria's reign to replace a more humble building, he saw a black and white cross-terrier cocking its leg against a tombstone in the disused graveyard.

"Gerroff!" he shouted.

The dog finished what it was doing and followed him at a safe distance until they reached a row of run down shops in the centre of which was a small Greek taverna. Dave had been there many times before. Thesus, the large sad faced owner, had never failed to give him a square meal and somewhere to sleep in return for doing a few odd jobs and even let him have a bath in an ancient zinc tub in an outhouse.

He went straight to the back of the premises where a double green gate opened into the taverna's yard. He pushed on the gate but it only gave enough for him to see that it was padlocked on the inside.

He shambled round to the front of the shops and looked through one of the taverna's windows. With sinking heart he saw chairs stacked on tables, and no sign of life. There was a notice on the inside of the window which he read in an undertone: "Due to the death of the proprietor this restaurant is closed. The family thanks the many customers who have expressed their sympathy."

Dave stared blankly at the stacked chairs. Thesus had been a friendly face in an unfriendly world.

A young man emerged from the kitchen at the back of the shop and waved for Dave to go away. A woman Dave recognised as Thesus's wife, now his widow, appeared behind the man, and then they both disappeared back into the kitchen.

The dog from the graveyard started sniffing round the taverna door. Dave raised his arm in a threatening gesture.

"Gerroutofit!" he shouted.

The dog stopped sniffing and wagged its tail. Dave picked up a half brick that was lying in the gutter. Thesus might be dead but he wasn't going to have a stray dog fouling the taverna door. Experience had taught Dave that stray dogs ran when someone picked up a brick. This one didn't. It just cocked its head to one side.

Dave hated stray dogs. They fouled shop entrances where he sometimes had to spend a night, and they ate good food from waste bins, but this dog didn't behave like a stray. It brought back unwanted memories of better times when he had owned such a pet.

He aimed the brick to just miss it, cursed his softness and shambled off back to the rear of the shops. There would be bins worth investigating there. The dog followed him.

The young man he had seen in the taverna was opening the green gate. Dave recognised him now as Thesus's son whom he had seen once or twice before.

"Please tell your mother. I'm very sorry. A fine man your father," Dave said.

The son paused holding the gate and snapped, "Get going! There's nothing for you here. My father's dead—and take that flee-ridden mongrel with you."

Before Dave could protest that it wasn't his dog a woman's strident voice called out something in Greek. The son reluctantly returned to the kitchen. Dave waited to see what was happening, and the dog started investigating forbidden territory in the yard.

A face appeared momentarily at the kitchen window; then, a few minutes later, the son came out carrying two parcels, approached Dave, and said, "My Mother wants you to have these. Now go, and take your dog with you—and don't come back."

Dave took the parcels, thanked the son, and silently blessed the matriarchy of this Greek household.

Once out on the street again he examined the parcels. One had been carefully wrapped and felt like a bundle of clothes. The other was a cardboard box, secured with adhesive tape, and emitting a strong smell of Geek cooking. The dog jumped up excitedly. Dave knocked it down roughly, aimed a half-hearted kick in its direction, and told it to go home.

Although very hungry he decided his first priority was to find somewhere to spend the night now that the Taverna's yard was out of bounds. The light was fading and he didn't relish entering back streets he didn't know in the dark.

After walking aimlessly for a time he arrived back at the church he had passed earlier. The grounds were as large as a small park, less than half of which was graveyard. And, almost hidden by the Church was what appeared to be a garden tool shed. The area was certainly extensive enough to justify a ride-on mower and a few power tools although the general condition of the graves left a lot to be desired.

He walked in through the open gates to investigate. The shed was what it appeared to be, and only a flimsy padlock secured the door. An ideal place to spend the night, Dave decided, and looked around for a suitable spot to eat.

He selected a horizontal gravestone hidden from the road by sprawling laurel bushes and read the almost obliterated engraving on it: 'In memory of William James Johnson a beloved husband and father born 1755 died 1801, and Elizabeth Jane Johnson beloved wife and mother born 1760 died 1828.'

"Lucky sods," he said, sat down and opened the box that Thesus's widow had given to him.

The box was packed with six dispensable fast-food containers, an assortment of fresh fruit, and a knucklebone wrapped in Clingfilm. On one of the containers was scribbled, 'Bone is for your dog.'

"Stupid woman," Dave muttered and laid the bone beside him on the stone.

At the sound of Dave's voice the dog appeared from behind a hideous stone angel about to ascend to heaven, sat down at his feet, and stared pathetically at him.

"Not a hope Spot," he said. The name had come from his subconscious, and sent a shiver down his spine, but the dog appeared to approve of its new handle and wagged its tail vigorously.

Dave opened two of the containers. There was enough moussaka in them to last him a day. He looked in the other four and they were equally well filled.

The bone ceased to appear appetising and he threw it to Spot.

He had just finished eating the contents of the first container, and was peeling an overripe banana, when a man in his early thirties wearing a sports coat, dog collar, and cords, came walking across the graveyard.

"Good evening reverend," Dave said.

"Is that your dog?" the Vicar asked, pointing in the direction of some bushes.

"No!" Dave replied, and, as if on cue, Spot appeared carrying a partially chewed knucklebone which he dropped at Dave's feet.

"He appears to know you well," the Vicar said.

"He can smell the food. He's been following me, all day," Dave replied, stretching the truth a little.

The Vicar bent down to see if Spot had a collar and was rewarded with a rumbling growl.

He straightened up abruptly and said, "I see! When you've finished your banana will you please move on and take him with you."

"Yes Reverend," Dave replied.

There was no point in being uncivil. The Vicar might come back if he were, and find him in the shed. He left the graveyard ahead of the Vicar, disposed of the banana skin and empty fast-food container in a nearby litterbin, and set of at a purposeful pace.

By taking a series of left turns, and slowing down after the first, he succeeded in arriving back at the graveyard twenty-five minutes later.

It was dark, and there were no lights in the church or annexe buildings, so he made his way straight to the hut. The padlock was as flimsy as it looked and offered no resistance to the old screwdriver he carried in one of his many pockets. The interior of the hut was dry and the floor concrete. He chased Spot out and pulled the door to, wedging it at the bottom with a piece of wood.

He slept well that night, too well. The sun was doing its best to stream through the dust and cobwebs on the hut's only window when he was wakened by Spot barking outside.

He heard the Vicar say, "It's that tramp's dog. I expect he's in there."

"More likely left with my tools," a second voice said.

"Why are vergers always so suspicious?" the Vicar replied.

Dave eyed the mower that was parked against the back wall. The blades were rusty, the four-stroke engine was covered in dust, but otherwise it appeared to be in good shape. On the wall opposite to the cobweb covered window was a well-equipped tool rack donated by a parishioner in the hope of encouraging the Verger to maintain the mower.

Dave pushed opened the door, and said, "I'm not a thief."

The Vicar and the Verger both took a step back "You're trespassing," the verger snapped.

"No sweat, I'm leaving," Dave answered, and went back into the hut to collect his belongings.

The Verger turned to the Vicar and said, "We can't just let him go. The place will be swarming with vagrants if we do."

"Hardly," the Vicar replied.

"And what about the padlock?"

"A few pence, and no real harm done."

"It's the principle of the thing," the Verger objected.

"What do you suggest?"

"At least make him pay for it?"

"That's absurd. He won't have two pennies to rub together."

"Some of these beggars do very well," the Verger objected.

"We can hardly search him."

"Call the police on your mobile," the Verger suggested.

At the word police Dave switched into the conversation; he was used to being talked about as if he weren't there, but that didn't mean that he wasn't listening.

"I could cut the grass round the graves," he suggested.

"I'm afraid the mower doesn't work," the Vicar said.

"I'm good with engines. There're enough tools on the bench," Dave replied, waving in the direction of the shed window.

"Very well, we'll settle for that, but don't let your dog foul the graveyard," the Vicar agreed.

"You can't just leave him with all those tools. They're my responsibility," the Verger said.

"So is keeping the graveyard tidy, and just look at it. I'll be responsible for anything that goes missing while this man is here. You have enough to worry about already," the Vicar retorted.

The Verger looked disparagingly at Dave, shrugged his shoulders and walked away.

"I think I may have a problem with my parishioners so don't let me down," the Vicar warned Dave.

"I'm no thief," Dave protested again.

"But you've been in prison."

"You think?"

"One gets to know in my calling. I was once a prison chaplain; what were you in for?"

Dave was silent for a full half minute before replying, "GBH! Some bastard seduced my wife. I caught them at it."

"You assaulted your wife?"

"No, the scumbag she was with. Hospitalised him for a month; nearly a week in intensive care."

The Vicar looked at him quizzically. "You suspected or you came home unexpectedly?" he asked.

"Came home unexpectedly." Then, when the Vicar said nothing, Dave added, "I cracked. I'm not a violent man. It was just with my bare hands; no knife; no boot in; nothing like that."

"Where is your wife now?"

"Disappeared with our two kids."

"Have you tried to trace them?"

"What's the point?  It's too late now anyway. Look at me."

"Have you no purpose in life?"

"None, I should have killed him. Murder gets more kudos inside than GBH."

"You don't really mean that. But first things first; we must find you some better clothes and a bed for the night. It will take a couple of days at least to tidy up this place. What's in the large parcel?"

"Clothes, they belonged to a Greek twice my size. His widow gave me them."

The Vicar thought for a moment, then said, "We have a jumble sale coming up soon. We might find something in what we've accumulated already. A fair exchange for what you have there."

"So that's the deal. I tidy up the graveyard. You don't go to the police?" Dave said.

"In a nutshell, yes."

"I'd have to sleep in the shed."

"That wouldn't do."

"I've no money."

"I'll arrange for your keep, but I would prefer if you didn't tell anyone in the Congregation about your incarceration."

"What about Spot?"

"I'll take him to the RSPCA."

Dave hesitated, then asked, "Can I keep him? Nobody would mind him sleeping in the shed. He wouldn't eat much, and the Verger would have a guard for his tools."

"I thought you said it wasn't your dog."

"It isn't but they lock strays up in a cage. He doesn't deserve that. He hasn't committed GBH."

"Very well, but we'll have to work out how you pay for his keep," the Vicar replied, and added: "There are plenty of odd jobs need doing about the place."

Next morning the Vicar and the Verger arrived simultaneously at the Church grounds.

"I can't see your tramp," the Verger said, unable to stop a note of triumph creeping into his voice; but as he spoke Spot appeared from under some shrubs, and Dave's head above them.

"Morning Vicar," Dave said. "This is going to take a lot longer than a couple of days."

"We'll play it by ear," the Vicar replied.

So, two days stretched out to a week, and a week to a month. The improvement in the graveyard received commendation from the whole of the small Congregation. Some members even gave plants from their gardens for the new flowerbeds alongside the main path.

Then, one morning, Dave arrived to find the graveyard desecrated. Gravestones had been covered with graffiti and some had even been smashed. Branches of bushes had been broken and the gates taken.

A terrible anger overwhelmed Dave. He sat down on a gravestone that had escaped the vandals' attention and gripped the edge to control his shaking. He didn't hear the Vicar approaching with the Verger and started violently when the Vicar said, "It appears that they've left your table untouched."

"Left what?"

"Your dining table," the Vicar replied, pointing to the inscription on the gravestone.

"When the worthy William Johnson was interred a man of your standing would have been shipped to the colonies for showing such disrespect," the Verger added.

"In that case the lot that did this would have danced on the gallows," Dave replied with a wave of his arm.

"Are you sure that your outrage isn't more to do with seeing something you have accomplished desecrated than anything else?" the Vicar asked.

Dave didn't answer.

"Did they get the tools?" the Verger asked.

"No, Spot saw to that," the Vicar replied.

Dave looked around. "Where's Spot now?" he asked.

"In the Rectory, a bit bruised but otherwise okay."

"I'll fucking kill 'em."

"Leave retribution to God and the law, and there's no need to revert to prison vernacular," the Vicar said.

"Sorry! I don't usually swear in front of reverends and women."

"Apology accepted. It looks as if you'll be here for some time clearing this mess."

"What's the point? It'll only happen again."

"It might, and then it might not if we improve security," the Vicar suggested.

Dave shook his head. "I was an Agent on building sites before they banged me up, and fences didn't keep them off the sites."

"It would deter them," the Verger said.

"All the parks in this neighbourhood have been vandalised. Haven't you noticed? If you don't have the community with you you're on to a looser," Dave said.

"So you don't think we have the Community with us?" the Vicar asked.

"Do you?" Dave replied.

The Vicar didn't answer.

Dave continued: "I've paid off my debt so I'll collect Spot and be on my way."

Still the Vicar was silent.

Dave turned and walked slowly to the gate. He had just reached it when he heard the Verger say, "The police rang before we came out.

They think they know who did this. If they catch the young hooligans I hope they lock them up for a long time."

"Do you think that will do much good?" the Vicar asked.

"A spell behind bars would do them no harm!" the Verger replied.

Dave stopped, the sound of a cell doors being slammed shut ringing in his head. Slowly he walked back to the Vicar.

"You could try employing young offenders working off their Community Service. There are plenty of local lads doing that," he said.

"You couldn't. What would the Congregation think?" the Verger asked.

Dave ignored him and continued, "If we made a small park for mothers with their kids, and pensioners, it might work. We could clear the graves. No one has been buried here for a hundred years."

The Vicar shook his head. "Not the graves," he said. Then an idea occurred to him. "More than half the site isn't graveyard and the Vicarage vegetable garden backs onto it. I'm sure the Church authorities would agree to us using that."

"And who's going to supervise these tearaways?" the Verger asked.

"They'll come with supervision, but Dave will be here," the Vicar replied, and then turning to Dave, added, "This should give you a purpose in life. What do you say?"

Dave said nothing.

"What street cred has a tramp with these tearaways?" the Verger asked scornfully.

"More than you could know," Dave retorted and walked away.

"Where are you off to?" the Vicar called out.

"To get the gates back," Dave replied.

# THE LAST KISS

Some kids keep hamsters, others tropical fish. Tony kept insects, not common insects but large tropical ones, especially spiders. So he spoke with some authority when he said, "That's not a real tarantula, it's a mega common house spider."

"It's a tarantula. I found it in a bunch of bananas," his cousin James protested, and quickly put the lid back on the small cardboard box as the last two guests for the family gathering arrived in the hallway.

It was Tony's parent's tenth wedding anniversary and they had arranged a family party more as a 'told you so' gesture to their nearest and dearest who said the marriage wouldn't last, than any wish to meet their disapproving relations en masse. The hundred percent acceptance of the invitations was partly due to the desire of those attending to see the latest addition to the house, a conservatory with heated pool, and partly to the reputation of Tony' father as a liberal host with the wine.

Tony hated any gatherings at which aunts and uncles were present, especially the over effusive Aunt Gloria who kissed everyone she met, including him. He and James intended to slip away upstairs to be with his insects as soon as they could do so unnoticed.

The last two guests joined the seven uncles and six competitively dressed aunts who were already sipping wine while they tried to outdo each other in describing their achievements since they last met. Tony was relieved to see that Aunt Gloria, whose arrival he had managed to avoid, had been cornered by Vernon while her husband and two other uncles expanded on their golfing achievements.

Vernon accounted for the odd number of guests. His ex-partner had gone on holiday with a girl friend the previous winter, met a bronzed Swiss skiing instructor and failed to return home. This left Vernon in a position to circulate freely, something that he had always done anyway.

Piqued at Tony' disdainful dismissal of his find, James, in a moment of weakness, responded to his mother who had been beckoning to him from across the room. He pushed the box into Tony's hands. "Hang onto this, mum's calling," he said and made his way through Aunts and Uncles as Tony' father turned up the background music and called for everyone to dance.

"This is James, hasn't he just grown?" his mother said in her shrill monotone to the couple whose company she was monopolising.

James gave them a sickly smile and just managed to stop himself from saying, "They didn't expect me to shrink."

Meanwhile Tony, who was now standing alone in the doorway regretting his offhand dismissal of his mate's find, suddenly felt vulnerable in the presence of so many grown up relations. He waved to James indicating that he was going upstairs. Too late he realised his mistake.

"What's that box Tony's waving?" Emily's asked her son, raising her voice to a pitch that could be heard all round the room above the music.

Vernon turned to see what was happening. The cornered Gloria grabbed the opportunity, gulped down her third glass of Chardonnay, pushed Vernon aside and called across the room, "Tony! My favourite nephew! Where have you been? Come and give Auntie Gloria a great big kiss." Then she wove her way elegantly through the dancing couples in the direction of the door.

"Lucky little sod," Uncle Vernon muttered under his breath.

Tony, now the focal point of everyone's attention, turned bright red as, incapable of moving, he gripped James's cardboard box and awaited the inevitable, his eyes switching back and forth between the luscious pink lips puckering up in readiness and the massive cleavage into which his face was about to be buried. James, who had also suffered the humiliation many times, watched, relishing every moment.

It probably took Gloria less than half a minute to reach Tony but to him it was an eternity before two arms encircled him and his face was buried in a smothering embrace of blouse, bosom and bra. Then a juicy kiss was planted on his forehead and a voice above his head said, "Isn't he just too cute!"

There the torture should have ended but the Chardonnay was having its effect and, instead of releasing Tony, Gloria held him at arms length and, teasing him, said, "Now, how about giving Aunt Gloria a real kiss!"

Taking her literally, and ready to do anything to escape, Tony pushed the cardboard box up the front of his 'T' shirt, flung his arms round her neck and, pulling himself up, gave her a resounding smacker full on the lips.

"My! You are getting a big boy," Gloria gasped, taking a step back smoothing her blouse to hide her confusion.

Tony didn't hang around. He turned and fled into the hall followed by the laughter of his aunts and uncles and Vernon's, "Well done lad!"

It wasn't until he stopped at the foot of the stairs and looked back to see if James was following that he remembered the cardboard box. He pulled it out from under his 'T' shirt and one glance confirmed his worst fears; it was flattened and there was no sign of the spider.

James crossed the room at a leisurely pace, followed by his mother who felt she owed it to her son to protect him from her sister-in-law. He smiled demurely at Gloria as he gave her a wide berth.

"Was it a sloppy one?" he asked Tony who was wiping his mouth on his sleeve.

"Shut it!" Tony replied.

"Is that my box? Where's my tarantula?" James gasped as he saw what Tony was clutching.

"Dunno."

"You've lost my tarantula!" James shouted.

"A tarantula's escaped!" The arachnophobic Aunt Emily squeaked and collapsed onto the hall seat.

"Is it on you?" James asked.

"I had the box up my shirt, but I'm sure it's not there," Tony said, pulling up the shirt while James made a close examination.

"Perhaps the lid came off when Aunt Gloria grabbed you. Look, there's the lid on the floor by the door!"

For a few seconds neither spoke; then James said, "I bet the spider's on Aunt Gloria!" and rushed into the lounge followed more slowly by a cautious Tony.

Gloria was now in the middle of the room dancing with Vernon who had grabbed her before she had recovered from the shock of being kissed by Tony and there, on top of her piled up coiffeur, James saw his spider.

"Look!" he shouted.

"Where?" Tony asked.

"On Aunt Gloria's head."

Gloria stopped dancing and turned to James. "What's on my head?" she asked.

"My tarantula," James replied.

"That's not funny," Gloria snapped.

"It's only a mega house spider," Tony added, in an attempt to be helpful.

"It's huge," Vernon said, looking at the spider which, at that moment, showed no inclination to move.

All eyes turned in Gloria's direction and Emily, who had recovered sufficiently to come back into the room, collapsed into Vernon's arms.

Gloria cautiously raised her hand and touched arthropod, then gave a strangled scream and swept it off her head, doing untold damage to her hairdresser's masterpiece as she did so.

Unfortunately the spider had already attached a strand of web to her hair in preparation for descending from its rather prominent perch so, instead of being hurled across the room, it swung out and back again frantically spinning a strand of web before disappearing into the gaping chasm of Gloria's cleavage.

Without a moment's hesitation Uncle Vernon dropped Aunt Emily and plunged his hand down after the spider which he managed to grab before it had found a hiding place in the vicinity of Gloria's bra; an act of gallantry that earned him a round of applause from the company, and a resounding slap in the face from Gloria which made him drop the spider on the recumbent Emily.

James grabbed the spider, and was hesitating, uncertain what to do about his mother whom he had seen faint many times before, when his father appeared and he decided the best policy was to disappear.

"I bet she never kisses us again," Tony whispered as he, James and the tarantula made a strategic retreat to Tony's room.

# Tales From Lower Moss Village

# DAVID AND GOLIATH

Bill Greenwood, a wiry, weather beaten dairy farmer in his forties, pushed open the door of the Lower Moss Village post office shop with his foot and entered carrying a pile of egg trays. Ignoring the small queue of villagers, he dumped them on the counter, and said, "Not more than three days old. Ethel can let you have more if you need them." He turned to go but found his way blocked by the substantial figure of Jenny Golightly, president of the local Women's Institute.

"Something has to be done about Lower Meadow Farm," she boomed.

"Well, the likes of I can't afford it," he replied. "Eight hundred acres of good land; must be worth a million or two, and a sight more for them developer types."

"That's the point. It's been on the market ever since old Seth died nearly two years ago because not one of you farmers round here can afford to buy it; and with the old farmhouse standing empty too."

"So what's changed?"

"Someone's made an offer."

"I ain't heard nowt."

"I only heard yesterday from someone I know on the County Council. It's not public knowledge yet."

"Some pop star who wants a country retreat I suppose," Megan, the postmistress, suggested.

"Worse! A leisure company wants to set up a theme park."

"Does the Parish Council know?"

"I spoke to the Parish Clerk. She hadn't heard anything and rang the County Council. They told her that an enquiry had been made about a project on the site but, until they received a planning application, the possibility of a change in use was pure speculation."

"They can't do that," Bill said. "It's greenbelt."

"It isn't; and they can. I've checked. Something has to be done before matters get out of hand," Jenny Golightly replied.

"So what's the Parish Council doing about it?" Megan said. "Nothing as usual I suppose."

"Quite!" Jenny Golightly boomed. "I spoke to our worthy Chairperson and she said they could do nothing until they had received copies of a planning application from the County Council; by which time it'll be too late so I've booked the Village Hall for Friday evening for an action meeting. I've had leaflets printed that I'm distributing in the village. I'll leave some here and Bill, you take a bunch too; do the farms, houses and cottages roundabout."

Bill needed no persuading as his property and Lower Moss Farm were on opposite sides of the road into the village.

By Friday evening rumours had spread that the County Council was also considering applications for a holiday camp or perhaps eco-houses to be built on the site. Jenny Golightly suspected that Bill might have started these. Whether that was so or not the combined rumours had the desired effect and, on Friday evening, the Hall was packed with villagers, farmers and residents from the expensive peripheral properties; a community united in one cause.

On the stage, seated at a long table facing down the Hall, were Jenny Golightly who had elected herself as Chairperson of the meeting, the Local Vicar, the Methodist Minister, Bill Greenwood and Val Hawthorne, licensee of 'The Farmer's Arms.' Megan had declined because of her position as postmistress, a nicety which, as someone pointed out, never interfered with her ability to disseminate news and rumours.

Jenny Golightly called the meeting to order, explained the situation and asked for comments. The Chairperson of the Parish Council immediately jumped up at the front of the Hall and tried to explain that there was nothing the Council, or anyone, could do until a planning application had been lodged.

She was greeted with a chorus of, "Sit down, sit down," which was silenced by Bill thumping the table and shouting above the noise, "You all know me and where my farm be. I say we form a pressure group like you read about in the papers to find out what's going on."

"Hear, hear! Villagers against unwanted developments," somebody from one of the expensive properties called back.

Shouts of approval from all over the Hall greeted the suggestion and Jenny Golightly grabbed the opportunity to speak. "Great idea," she boomed, "But let's be specific, holiday camps and eco-housing schemes are just wild rumours. 'Villagers Against Theme Parks, V.A.T.P.,' that will get us going and we can take more onboard if we have to."

The Vicar looked uneasy and said, "I think we should wait until we know more," and the Chairperson of the Parish Council jumped up again but got no further than saying, "This is a Parish Council matter," before she was shouted down.

Jenny Golightly stood up and called for silence, then said, "Can I have a show of hands for Villagers Against Theme Parks." The hands of two thirds of those present shot up, and most of the remaining third slowly followed suit as she ran a disconcerting eye over the assembly before calling out, "Any against?" The six members of the Parish Council and the local solicitor raised their hands.

"I take it we're agreed. Now we need five or six volunteers to form an action committee," she boomed.

There was an awkward silence until Bill stood up and said, "I volunteer so that makes two, me and Jenny." Then he turned to the two ministers and Val and asked, "What about you?"

After a moment's hesitation Val agreed but the clergy didn't think that the church authorities would be happy for them to be on an unofficial committee. Bill turned to the room, "What about you Charlie? Your pig farm's next to Lower Meadow?"

Charlie agreed reluctantly as all eyes turned on him; then the two Johnson brothers, who owned the local agricultural plant hire business, volunteered.

Events moved faster than expected and on the Monday following the meeting the local postman told Megan that he had seen a green Bentley parked in the yard of Lower Meadow Farm.

Megan immediately contacted Val, the fit, forty plus, licensee of the Farmers Arms who was in jeans and sweatshirt taking a delivery of keg beer. Val wasted no time in contacting the Council but either her contact wouldn't or couldn't tell her anything. She then spoke to the other members of the V.A.T.P committee but, like her, they were busy and, apart form Bill Greenwood, could see no point in forming a deputation to visit the farm on the assumption that the visitor was a theme park representative.

When Val contacted Bill on his mobile to tell him that the other members of VATP were not prepared to meet the owners of the Bentley he was on his way to spread a load of ripe cow manure on his end field across the road from Lower Meadow Farm's 'Hundred Acre Meadow'. After only a moment's hesitation he drove to the farm and deposited the load across the entrance to the yard where the Bentley was still parked. "Welcome to Lower Moss Village," he called out as he swung his tractor round and set off back home for another load.

In the following days rumours spread through the village that a Bentley covered in cow dung had been seen parked in the County Council car park and of meetings in the Council Offices to discuss the matter. However, by Thursday evening, there hadn't even been an unofficial complaint to the Parish Clerk and the cow dung at Lower Meadow Farm remained as dumped, except for where the Bentley had driven through it.

Finding silence more worrying than confrontation, Jenny Golightly brought the meeting of the 'V.A.T.P.' forward to eleven-thirty on Friday morning, before the lunchtime customers started to arrive, so she could contact the Council in the afternoon if need be.

Charlie, the local pig farmer, was the first to arrive straight from the piggery, a burly man in his fifties wearing a checked shirt, aged tweed jacket and well worn jeans. Five minutes later Bill appeared followed closely by the young Johnson brothers in overalls embellished with the logo 'JOHNSON BROTHERS PLANT HIRE' over the logo of a combine-harvester. Finally the imposing Jenny made her entry wearing a dark jacket, cream blouse, pleated skirt and 'sensible shoes'.

After buying their drinks individually the group assembled at a window table where Val was within easy call of the bar.

Ray, the elder Johnson brother, was the first to speak. "You shouldn't have done it Bill," he said. "Not without us all agreeing. You've made your point. Now I reckon you should shift it."

"Worried about losing that Council contract?" Bill countered.

Charlie held up his hand. "No need for that. Thee mustn't get personal. This is a village matter."

"That's all very well for you," Frank, the younger Johnson brother, chipped in. "You don't sell your pigs to the Council. We've made our point and now it should be cleared up before matters escalate. What do you say, Jenny?"

"Clear it up; be damned! I say well done Bill, and I reckon Charlie here should add a load of pig manure to it."

Charlie's shifted uneasily on his chair at the suggestion. "That might be counter productive," he replied. "I say we just leaves it as it is and until the Council gets round to moving it. No one's living at the farm."

"The muck's on private land," Val said. "This isn't a Council matter. I agree that we've made a point and Bill aught to pick it up. I'm only surprised that someone hasn't shifted it to use on their garden."

Emboldened by the support he had received from the formidable Jenny Golightly, Bill retaliated, "Never! As Val here says, there's nowt the Council can do. It's not on road and if them leisure company guys come after me for having to drive their Bentley through cow shit I'd tell 'em I'd go to the national press; it being a sort of David and Goliath thing. The press would love it. Them leisure guys wouldn't. We're ahead one nil."

"This isn't a soccer match," Charlie said, alarmed at the thought of the national press swarming over the village, but Jenny Golightly boomed, "I like it! I like it! David one Goliath nil! Let's go to the press now and make it two nil!"

There was a lull in the conversation while the rest of the group took in what Jenny had just suggested. Then Charlie, who had been looking out of the window to avoid Jenny's enquiring stare, saw a green Bentley pull up outside the pub.

"I think Goliath has just arrived," he announced.

The six watched through the window as a smartly dressed man in his thirties got out of the Bentley and walked to the pub door. By the time he strode into the now silent bar Val was behind the counter and the five were seated round the table apparently engrossed in conversation.

The man looked round the bar, saw that the clientele present consisted of the group of five, and two regulars by the fire, and ordered, "A tonic, ice and slice for me and the same again for everyone else."

There was a murmur of thanks before he continued, "Which of you is Bill?"

There was silence for a moment before Bill answered, "Me! So what?"

The stranger knocked back his tonic and replied, "I'm Fred, the farmer who's bought Lower Meadow Farm. I came to thank you for the manure!"

There was gasp from Bill followed by a slightly longer silence while Fred waited for some comment. Receiving none, he continued, "Kind thought, but I'm afraid I always use slurry."

"Slurry! Rotting cow effluent! Stinks for miles! Shouldn't be allowed!" Jenny Golightly boomed.

"So you're not from the leisure company!" Bill said, having eventually found his voice again.

"Certainly not! I sold one of my farms to them for several million— a much better site for a theme park. Now, about the manure, I appreciate the thought but, as I said, I only use slurry so I had it returned to your yard, plus a load of slurry you might like to try out. I usually have surplus."

"To my yard!" Bill gasped. "Yard's at side door of house opposite milking parlour. Dung heap's round back of farm!"

"My man thought it best dropped in the yard in case you didn't want the lots mixed. It shouldn't be difficult to shovel up. I must rush now. Got three hundred head of livestock arriving shortly. Let me know if you'd like another load of slurry."

No one spoke as Fred strode out of the pub, but while they watched the Bentley disappearing down the High Street. Val remarked, "I make that, David one Goliath two!"

# A SMALL FAMILY FIRM

Travelling home by train after a rare visit to the city Val Forrest was fortunate in finding an unoccupied window seat. As licensee of the Farmer's Arms in Lower Moss Village she had to make the occasional visit to the city on business and was always relieved to be returning home.

Wearing a sage green trouser suit with all five buttons of the long jacket done up, and the top two of the cream blouse underneath undone to allow the collar to stand proud of the jacket, she didn't look like the no-nonsense landlady of the Farmer's Arms that the inhabitants of Lower Moss Village knew.

She had just relaxed when a man, stopped at the empty seat next to her and enquired, "Anyone sitting here?"

"No," Val replied and moved her handbag and shopping so it was safely tucked between her and the side of the carriage, not because he looked threatening, more of an instinctive action; it wasn't like being on the local bus where she would know most of the passengers. The man was an insignificant character in his mid-fifties, of small build with dark thinning hair, pallid face and expressionless blue eyes.

His grey trousers needed pressing and his open necked grey-green shirt looked crumpled. The old rough tweed jacket he wore had large pockets and was loosely buttoned up as if it were too big for him; probably bought in a charity shop, Val decided. She considered herself to be a good judge of character and this man looked as if he found life one long struggle. She decided he probably lived on his own in a run-down town flat and mentally named him Mr. Grey.

"Thank you. Trains are so crowded these days," Mr. Grey said as he sat down.

His manners belied his appearance but he didn't look like a commuter and Val was intrigued. "On holiday?" she asked.

"No! Business, I run a small family firm."

"Difficult time for small family firms, what with bad debts," Val ventured.

"No problem. We only take cash and credit cards."

"So do I," Val responded. It had now been a good many years since she had reluctantly accepted the inevitable. If a pub served food it had to accept credit cards.

Mr. Grey didn't reply. He fished a newspaper from an inner pocket of his jacket and turned to the sports page. It was obvious he had no desire to make conversation so Val found her copy of The People's Friend and started to read too.

The train was well on its way to the first stop when a youth in his late teens came unsteadily down the carriage followed by a girl of about the same age. The youth was dressed conventionally in the latest designer jeans, monogrammed shirt opened to reveal a hairy chest and two rings in each ear; at six feet tall and well built he was an imposing figure. The girl sported red, green and black hair, heavy makeup, jeans of the same pattern as the youth's and an expensive embroidered blouse undone sufficiently to reveal a good cleavage. They had obviously been drinking.

He stopped by Mr. Grey. "My girl wants a seat," he said arrogantly. He was handsome, and he knew it, but his features were marred by a half sneer that made his mouth lopsided. His obvious intention was to show off for the benefit of the girl.

Mr Grey didn't look up from his paper, which was a mistake. The youth grabbed him by an arm and hauled him out of the seat. He staggered into the youth, knocking him onto two men sitting the other side of the isle where he struggled to stand up before the men pushed him roughly to his feet. The loss of face was apparently too much for the youth and he made to hit Mr. Grey. The girl screamed and grabbed his arm but he shook her off so violently that she fell onto the laps of two smartly dressed women in the seat behind Val.

The girl let out a torrent of abuse and scrambled to her feet, leaving the two women dishevelled and breathless.

As a licensee, Val had dealt with situations like this in the pub but she was not on home territory and she wasn't sure what course of action she should take, if any. She stood up and looked round for Mr. Grey and was just in time to see him making for safety down the carriage, barging clumsily into people who had stepped into the aisle to see what the commotion was about, before disappearing into the next carriage.

The passengers in the vicinity of the incident appeared to have forgotten Mr. Grey, if they had noticed him at all, and the two women in the seat behind were pouring abuse at the girl who was giving back as good she got. One of the two men the youth had fallen onto was standing in the aisle weighing up the youth. The man was in his thirties and the smart suit he was wearing didn't hide his muscular build.

"Got a problem?" the youth sneered and stepped forward, bumping into the man.

The confrontation was beginning to look ugly but before Val could put her experience of such situations to use the train started to slow down.

"Our station!" the girl shouted and grabbed the youth by an arm. To everyone's surprise he didn't react violently but followed her as they barged their way down the crowded aisle, in the opposite direction to that taken by Mr. Grey.

"Someone should report them to the police," one of the women said as she smoothed down her blouse and tidied her hair.

"What's the point? The police wouldn't be interested. What crime have they committed apart from causing a disturbance?" the man, still seated across the aisle to Val, said.

"That lout threatened me and if we could find the old man he pulled out of the seat we could have him for assault," the other man replied.

Val had a feeling that Mr. Grey wouldn't want to be involved and was about to say so when the train gave a jolt and started to move.

"Too late! There they are, the two of them hurrying down the platform," one of the women shouted.

Val looked out of the window just as they walked either side of Mr. Grey who wasn't hurrying and linked arms with him. Surely, she thought, they aren't going to mug him on the platform surrounded by all those bustling passengers making for the ticket office, and then she wondered if anyone would notice and if they did, would they want to get involved?

It was at that moment that one of the women behind her screamed, "My purse it's gone!" followed by her companion.

Val felt for her handbag; it was still safely tucked between her and the side of the carriage. Then the man who had been threatened shouted, "He's got my wallet," followed by his companion. Before many seconds had passed there was a chorus of voices up and down the carriage proclaiming losses.

Val looked out of the window again and was just in time to see Mr. Grey leave the platform with the young couple, and she could have sworn that all three of them were laughing.

As she told the regulars at the Farmer's Arms that night, and the police the following morning, it was then that she realised what Mr. Grey had meant by a small family firm taking only cash and credit cards.

# THE EGG BUS

Bill stopped his tractor in the road and looked across to Fred Jackson's distant fields full of hens scratching around. "A thousand head of beef cattle and now who knows how many thousand hens," he muttered. "It's not right; intensive farming, that's what it is an' the village could do without it."

He was about to set off again when a minibus driven by none other than Fred himself passed the tractor and turned into the lane down to the farm; except, it wasn't really a minibus, although Bill was sure he had seen something similar before. He worried about it all the way back to his farm and sent half a dozen hens squawking and flapping across the yard to the safety of the hay barn as he swung the tractor into the yard.

"What do you think you're doing, you great oaf!" Ethel shouted as she came to the door to see what was attacking her precious hens. "You nearly had some of my best layers then."

"It's those hens you bought cheap back of Christmas—they don't have no road sense," Fred retorted.

"They're still the best layers I've had so watch how you go."

Ethel kept around a hundred free-range birds which had the run of their dairy farm. She sold the eggs at the roadside, as a notice board announced, and supplied the village post office shop. However, in the winter she often didn't have enough eggs to satisfy both outlets, so, when she heard a rumour that the Postmistress had approached Fred Jackson, she bought forty 'on the point of lay' birds.

Bill clambered off the tractor muttering, "It were that Fred's fault. He's got me thinking. I've just seen him driving a minibus. Bussing in them illegal immigrant workers I reckon."

It only took Bill's visit to the Farmer's Arms for a pint that evening for the rumour to take hold.

Two days later it was the main topic of conversation in the WI, until the Postmistress arrived, late as usual. She had been asked to display a notice that the local bus service was being rerouted from the first of the following month because not enough village people used it.

"Of course we don't use it. By the time they get us into town it's time to come back for tea. There's plenty would use it if it ran at sensible times," old Mrs. Willowby said in the high-pitched voice she used when showing disapproval.

"Perhaps Mr. Jackson's setting up a village taxi business, not bussing foreign labour," someone suggested.

"Rubbish, it would never pay," Jenny Golightly, the formidable group chairperson boomed. "There's a perfectly adequate taxi firm this side of town for those who can afford it. He's up to something but it will be connected with farming; that's for sure. I'd say cheap foreign labour; doesn't have to be illegal."

It was nearly a week later when Fred Jackson contacted the Johnson brothers, who own the local agricultural plan hire business, to hire a muck spreader. It was their first business contact with him and Frank Johnson, the younger brother, decided to make the delivery himself.

As he drove down the lane to Lower Moss Farm he could see the minibus and recognised it immediately as a transporter vehicle used to take passengers and their luggage from airports to selected hotels. He deliberately drew up alongside it and jumped down from the driver's cab to have a look.

"My foreign workers' transport," Fred said with a laugh as he joined him.

"So it's true!"

"Of course not. My type of farming isn't seasonal. I have a well established workforce."

"You don't have anyone from the village working for you."

"I advertised, but no one from the village applied. I got plenty from other villages—some come from ten miles away; I suppose you'd call them foreign labour but I have no plans to bus them in."

"I think you should let the village know what you're up to. We're a very tight community."

"I agree it's time they knew. The idea will only work if you lot agree. Perhaps you could resurrect that committee you had to stop this farm from being sold for a theme park."

"Good thinking. Make it Friday at the Farmer's Arms unless you hear otherwise," Frank replied.

The other past members of the committee, Val the licensee of the Farmer's Arms, Jenny Golightly, Charlie the local pig farmer, and Frank's brother, all agreed immediately. Only Bill objected. "He's a right smooth talker. He'll have you all agreeing to things before we've even made our point; what we need is direct action," he protested.

"Any more of your direct action and you'll find yourself off the committee," Frank warned.

Eventually Bill agreed to attend, but it was not without misgivings on Frank's side that they parted. He would have been even less happy if he had called on Bill the following evening. Ethel had finished preparing their meal when she realised that Bill hadn't come in. Worried, because he was always ready for his food, she went looking for him and found him engrossed in painting 'KEEP VILLAGE JOBS FOR VILLAGE MEN' on boards he had nailed to fencing stakes.

"What do you think you're doing now?" she asked.

"When we've listened to all Fred's excuses for bussing in cheap foreign labour I'm going to put these in our field across the road from his place. Not being on his land he can't do nowt about it."

"I told you, you're paranoid. You don't know what he's going to say and if you put those notices up I'll be the first to knock them down; men indeed, what about us women? If you don't come in right now I'll give your meal to the dogs."

On Friday evening Bill, Charlie and the two Johnson brothers arrived in Bill's Land Rover. It had been Frank's idea to ask Bill to drive so there would be no risk of too much alcohol loosening his tongue. Jenny Golightly was already in the pub expounding to Val on the damage that foreign workers were doing to the British economy. "Where's Bill?" she boomed as three of the four men reached the bar.

"Dunno; he drove us here and it's not his round," Charlie replied, turning to stare at the closed door. He was about to go back out when Bill appeared triumphantly carrying one of his signs saying, 'KEEP VILLAGE JOBS FOR VILLAGE FOLKS.'

"You can put that away," Frank said, grabbing the sign and passing it over the bar to Val just as a vehicle drew up outside the pub.

"The cheek of the man—it's the minibus thing," Jenny Golightly boomed as she moved to where she could see out of the window.

The bar fell silent as the door opened and Fred appeared. "A tonic, ice and slice and I'll buy this round," he said.

Bill was the first to speak. "Don't think you can buy us with a round of drinks and a few soft words," he blustered.

"Let the man have his say," Jenny Golightly boomed.

"Thank you, I know Bill here doesn't approve of my farming methods although the Ministry of Agriculture and all concerned with animal welfare tell me that my methods are among the most humane they have come across."

"They're still not good farmyard hens," Bill blustered. "They don't even look like them."

"Of course my eggs may not taste quite the same as yours from hens that have feasted on fat dung heap worms but they're far above the average supermarket egg. That's where the transporter comes in. By the big supermarkets' standards my egg output is small, but I supply a lot of lesser outlets and local market stalls including the one in the town near here."

"You better not start supplying our post office shop," Bill interrupted. "That's my missus's territory."

"I can assure you I have no intention of undermining any existing local businesses. But I came hear to tell you about the transporter. I use vans for my egg deliveries—they slip easily in and out of congested markets, and a couple of weeks ago I saw that transporter for sale so I bought it. I happened to have heard that the village bus was about to be rerouted and it occurred to me that here was a dual-purpose vehicle. On the local town runs it could carry a few village folk as well as eggs. They would have to start early but that wouldn't worry country folk. It would pick them up again sometime mid-afternoon."

"That would need a special licence and qualified driver," Frank interjected.

"Nothing that can't be arranged."

There was complete silence for a moment before Jenny Golightly boomed, "Well I'll be damned, and after all those awful rumours! Wait till I tell the WI. I can say for certain that you'll have their full support."

"And you can be sure of that," Charlie added. "No one argues with Jenny."

"You're not planning to sell eggs to the folk on this egg bus?" Bill asked.

"He told you he's not selling local," Frank snapped.

Charlie laughed. "Bill's worried. His missus bought forty 'point of lay birds' dirt cheap at Littleford market back of Christmas."

"So what?" Bill retorted. "They're real farmyard hens. Best layers she's ever had."

Fred turned to him and said slowly, "That would be 28$^{th}$ November. I bet they're good layers. That guy lifted 200 of my new stock on the night of the 27$^{th}$ but we nabbed him the following week.

# THE WATER FEATURE

"Has he paid?" Ray Johnson asked his younger brother.

"Yes, no problem, but I'm glad it was his driver doing the digging. He's now threatening to sue the developer," Frank replied.

It was just over a week since Terrance Fiddler, the new owner of 'The Chestnuts' had called in at the Johnson Brothers' agricultural plant hire business to hire a digger.

"I only want the digger. I have my own driver," Fiddler had snapped when Frank quoted for a machine and driver.

"We normally supply a driver with our large diggers," Frank replied.

In riding breaches and hacking jacket the overweight, muscular Fiddler looked a menacing figure beside the slim built younger Johnson Brother.

"My man is perfectly capable of handling a digger," he said, and took a step closer to Frank.

Frank didn't move and asked, "What will you be excavating?"

"I can't see that's any business of yours, but if you must know, a few flowerbeds and a water feature in the garden on the west side of the house. So, when can I collect this digger?"

"We always deliver to site, Health and Safety, you know."

Fiddler's face started to turn crimson and, for a moment, Frank thought he was going to receive a mouthful of abuse. In the short time Fiddler had lived in the district his quick temper had become well known, but he controlled himself and said, "All right then, but remember I want it delivered, Monday morning, no later than eight."

At seven-fifty on Monday one of the Johnson Brothers' drivers arrived with the digger at the imposing entrance to 'The Chestnuts', a large property a mile out of the village. He dismounted and pressed the button on an intercom on one of the massive stone pillars that supported two black wrought iron gates decorated with a surfeit of red knobs, green leaves and gold arrowheads.

"Who's there?" a voice asked.

"Johnson's digger," the driver replied.

"Go up the drive and take the path off to the left shortly before you reach the house. Our driver will meet you there," the voice instructed and the gates slowly swung open.

The digger crunched its way up the loose pebble drive, one of Fiddler's vanities, and turned left onto an unmade path where the driver was waiting.

After satisfying himself that Fiddler's driver was familiar with handling heavy equipment and understood the controls on the hired model, Johnson Brothers' driver insisted on being driven to the site where the digger would be working.

'The Chestnuts' had originally been 'Hill Farm' and, as the name suggested, it commanded a fine view out over the village. A local property developer bought it when the family, who had owned it for over a century, ceased farming.

The dealer sold off all the land to Lower Meadow Farm except for four acres around the farmhouse and buildings. He then extended and converted the farmhouse and farm buildings into what he described as 'A fine freehold Country Residence with three reception rooms, large modern kitchen, five bedrooms, four en-suit, three car garage and stabling all set in four acres of garden and paddock'. However, due to a weakening local market for prestige properties, it had stood empty for nearly two years before Fiddler bought it at rather less than the developer had hoped to get.

The planned alteration to the garden was on the west side of the house where there was a large lawn running down to the boundary fence and on it the sites of flower beds, paths and the water feature had already been pegged out.

Satisfied that it was unlikely that Fiddler's driver would have any problems, Johnson Brothers' driver rang the Depot to say he was ready for someone to pick him up.

"The job shouldn't take too long," Fiddler's driver said as they sat in the digger waiting.

"You'd be into clay after five feet," Johnson's driver warned.

"Boss is having raised flower beds so I won't be going that deep except for the water feature."

"Where's that going?

"In the area marked out in the middle of the lawn."

"I'd say that was just about where the pigsties used to be. Not that they kept many pigs, but that'd be about the spot. Where's the water coming from?"

Fiddler's driver laughed. "You know my boss, or perhaps you don't, him being new here. He's always out to save a few pounds. He's on a metre so he's going to tap into an underground stream."

"You're joking. I've lived in the village all my life and I can tell you there's no underground streams round here."

"He reckons there is. He got someone, local water diviner fellow, to come and check over the site until he found water."

"Wouldn't be Twiggy Jones by any chance?"

"That'll be him, Gareth Jones. Came with a hazel twig which twitched when he walked over the lawn. Not that I believe in these things. Mark you, I think he was a bit put off when his stick twitched. He'd told boss that he didn't expect to find anything. Boss suggested it might be a well but twiggy fellow said he'd be surprised because it would have to be real deep and he reckoned the water he found was near the surface. He wanted to trace the source but boss had got all he wanted, and he was paying by the hour!"

Johnson's driver shrugged and said, "Twiggy's found plenty of water for folks over the years but I reckon he's wrong this time. He'd know there aren't any streams or wells here—that's why he'd be surprised. Anyway, go cautious like, we don't want our digger nose-diving into a disused well we don't know about. Take it easy, just in case. Here's my boss—just arrived to take me back."

Fiddler saw Frank arrive and went down to the site to meet him. "Worried that my driver can't cope," he snapped before Frank could say anything.

"No problem there. He'd have rung me if he were worried and I'd have been in contact. So this is where you're putting your fountain. It'll put your water bill up a bit I do reckon," Frank replied.

"Water feature and, if you must know, there's water underground here which I propose to tap into. I've had it checked."

"By a Gareth Jones," Johnson's driver explained.

Frank looked from his driver to Fiddler and said, "Twiggy's not often wrong but I'd be willing to bet that there's no underground stream anywhere on your grounds."

"Fifty quid?" Fiddler snapped.

Frank hesitated and Fiddler sneered, "Different when you've got to put your money where your mouth is!"

"Alright then, you're on; fifty quid that there's no well or stream within fifty metres of your water feature."

"Done! Now let my driver get on with digging the paths and flowerbeds. I'll ring you when we get to the water feature."

"Fifty quid! That is what he paid the Twiggy guy; you've got to hand it to my boss," Fiddler's driver whispered to Johnson's driver.

It was later in the day, when Frank was making the rounds of local farmers to find out what equipment they expected to be hiring in the month ahead, that he learned more about the water feature. He was having a cup of tea in Farmer Bill Greenwood's kitchen when the conversation turned to what Fiddler was doing with Hill Farm, as the locals still called it.

Bill told him that a landscape gardener he knew had been called in to give an estimate for re-laying out a lawn area on the west side with flowerbeds and a water feature. She, the landscape gardener, had seen Twiggy dowsing and he had definitely located water, which worried her in case there might be an old well. Old wells on farms were often not capped securely and, in that location, it would have to have been at least fifty feet deep to have had any chance of reaching water.

"So he's hiring my digger to find it," Frank said, visualising his digger nose down in a well shaft.

"That would be too simple for the likes of he. The sod told my gardener friend her quote was too high. By that time he had the outline plan for the whole garden. He's using casual labour for the job, that's why he needs a digger. He's a right skinflint when you think how much he's worth."

Frank laughed. "Probably why the guy's so rich. But I still say there's no well or stream there, especially where he's putting that water feature; it's where the pigsties were. I hope I'm right—I'd hate to lose fifty quid to that guy."

Two days later an account customer contacted the Johnson Brothers to hire the digger and Frank decided to call at The Chestnuts to check how much longer the equipment was likely to be required on site. Knowing Fiddler's reputation he expected a hostile reception and a barrage of complaints about the equipment, finishing with a demand for a discount. Instead he was welcomed by Fiddler who said, "Right on the dot. I was about to phone you. We're ready to dig out for the water feature and I thought you'd like to see your fifty quid going down the well, so to speak!"

Frank had to admit that whoever had been responsible for laying out the garden had done a first class job, and in a remarkably short time. The lawn had gone, except where the water feature was to be located, and the whole area had been graded to different levels with flowerbeds and rockeries separated by winding paths. Everywhere was ready for planting except the area round where the water feature was to be built. Fiddler's driver obviously knew exactly what he was doing and Frank made a mental note to obtain his name and address.

The digger was in position and ready to start digging when Frank and Fiddler arrived at the site.

"Now to open up the well. You can pick up your digger tomorrow midday. I'll have your check ready less the fifty quid," Fiddler said and signalled to his driver to start digging.

After the top eighteen inches of grass and soil had been systematically removed, and there was no sign of water, Fiddler became impatient. He waved to the driver to switch off the engine then shouted, "Stop messing about, go in deep!"

The driver did as instructed and a jet of water shot several feet into the air. Fiddler gave shout of triumph. The driver stopped digging, jumped down onto the ground and looked at the waterspout. "You didn't warn me that there was a bloody water main there!" he called out to Fiddler.

"A what?" Fiddler gasped.

"A bloody water main!"

There was a moment's silence broken by one of the casual workers saying, "I reckon that be the supply to the old pig sties and barns like. They couldn't have removed it, just blanked off the end like. You can't trust them developers. I reckon your water meter'll be going round like a top."

That brought an immediate response from Fiddler. "Turn it off someone!" he shouted.

No one moved.

"Where's the stopcock?" he shouted at his driver.

"In the road!" the driver called back.

"Not that one. There must have been one for the farm buildings!"

"That might be anywhere. You'll have to see the Water Board and as like as not they didn't install it," the casual worker said.

Frank intervened. "Best turn the water off in the road as your driver suggested; then you could get Twiggy to trace the broken water pipe back to the house. I'll put the fifty quid you owe me onto the hire invoice."

*Tales Out of the Ordinary*

# A WEE TOAST TO THE SCENTED LADY

In the warmth of her bedroom Jenny Cameron gave Sandy one last lingering kiss. She ached for him to make love to her again, but knew he daren't. It was late and her father soon would be pedalling his aged bicycle up the glen on his way home from the bar in the village.

Outside the October mist hung low over the Highland muir, occasionally stirred into little eddies by a breeze from nowhere. The light from the Farmhouse windows was just a blur to anyone passing on the road winding down to the village.

Jenny wrapped her late mother's old muffler round Sandy's head and knotted it under his chin, "You'll be keeping that on. We dinna want the local assistant vet going down with pneumonia," she said.

The scent of jasmine enveloped him. "I didn't give you that perfume to put on your old muffler," he teased.

She kissed him again. "You ken well that father doesn't approve of me wearing scent so I put it on the muffler to remind me of you while I'm working on the farm. You best stuff it in a bag, soon as you get back or that auld biddy of a landlady will be spreading tales."

Sandy laughed. "If she smells it I'll say I met lovelorn Maggie on the muir."

Jenny frowned. "Now, dinna go mocking the spirits. It was in October on a night like this that she was lost. It's alright for the likes of you from the towns to mock but there's nae a man in the village over fifty, so they say, who hasn't seen her at least once—and a few of the lads too, only they won't admit it," Jenny chided.

"Old wives' tales," Sandy responded. "I bet you've never seen her."

"No woman's ever seen her. She seeks a man. Some say she's looking for her dead lover but others for the father who mortally wounded him. There have been a few men lost on the muir over the years who shouldn't have been."

"Do you think I'm handsome enough to qualify as her lover?"

Jenny laughed and kissed him. "Nae doubt at all and dinna be taking the short cut across the heather in this mist. Ring me the moment you reach the village."

Wisps of dank mist stretched their tentacles into the warmth as Jenny opened the farmhouse door and Sandy paused. "I'm not going to leave you here any longer. I love you and this is no place for a bonny girl like you. If your father won't agree we'll just up and get wed."

Jenny's eyes filled with tears. "Oh Sandy! If only—but look what the drink's done to him since mother died. What would it do to him if I left that soon after?"

"Soon after! It's two years since, and he'll mourn her for ever. Your brother's as good as running the farm now, he aught to be living here. It's time things were sorted. Next time I see your father half sober I'll tell him we're not waiting any longer." Sandy made to kiss her again, but she gently pushed him away.

"No! Go before he gets here. We dinna want another row like last time. It was the talk of the village."

"He started it, shouting out telling me to go back to the town where I belong and find a wife there."

"It was the drink talking. I promise I'll speak to him once more. It's better that we have his blessing. This is a small community and you're still a stranger, you'd get guy little sympathy if anything happened to him because I upped and went. And keep that muffler on, it's a cauld night."

Out on the muir the mist was playing all its tricks. It would lift to give visibility of fifty metres for a minute or two and then the damp grey blanket would descend again so it was hard to see five metres ahead. Sandy knew that Jenny was right, it would be worse than foolish to try to cross the two miles of peat bog and heather that stretched between the farmhouse and the edge of the village. He would have to walk the three and a half miles of road that wound through the glen.

He had not yet hardened to life in the mountains and it felt as if the dank mist was penetrating to the marrow of his bones. He pulled up the collar on his Barbour, flung the ends of the muffler over his shoulders so they hung like long grey locks of hair and strode into the night. A fit twenty-five, just short of six-foot-four tall and broad shouldered, he was a sight to frighten even Maggie.

He realised that by taking the longer way back to the village he was liable to meet Red Cameron weaving his way drunkenly on his bicycle so kept well to the left side of the road. He wasn't looking for trouble but if Red said anything he doubted if he could hold his tongue. He never ceased to wonder how such a man could father a girl like Jenny. True, she had inherited his hair colouring and quick temper, but not his terrible rages, and her freckled complexion was as fresh as the early spring pastures.

About a mile back along the undulating road Lofty and Shorty MacLean were approaching Red Cameron's farm in their old Ford van. They were on their way from Fort William to see their sister in the village, and arguing as they always did.

"I telt you to fill her up when you collected yon parcel from the station," Lofty said as he swerved to miss a cow that turned out to be a trick of the mist.

"That you didn't," Shorty retorted. "You just telt me to collect the parcel. The tank was full afore you took your Ethel to see her father."

"I telt you plain enough and now we'll like as not run out of petrol afore we get there. You should have seen it was nearly empty."

"It's nae my fault and this isn't a guid nicht to be stranded on the muir."

"Afraid you'll meet Maggie," Lofty mocked.

"It's nae laughing matter," Shorty retorted and turned to peer out of the side window.

It was at that moment they came up behind Sandy and passed him rather too close for comfort. Startled out of his reverie Sandy shook his fist and shouted after them, but the mist swallowed his words.

"Holy Mother did you see that?" Shorty gasped, recoiling from the window and grabbing Lofty's arm.

"Watch what you're doing or you'll have us in the ditch," Lofty shouted.

"But did ye nae see it?"

"See what?" Lofty asked.

"If it wasna Maggie herself I dinna ken what it was," Shorty replied.

Lofty glanced disparagingly at his brother. "Red Cameron has cattle on the muir. It would be one of them. We'll meet a few more afore the night's gone if we run out of bloody petrol. My God, this mist is thick. Where are we now?"

"This wasna one of Red's cattle. It was all of seven feet tall with grey hair hanging down its back."

"Maggie's nae feet tall and she never had grey hair."

"Two hundred and fifty years on the muir would turn anybody grey. It was Maggie; I tell you," Shorty protested.

"It was the mist. You'll be seeing Maggie in the van next. Look, there's the signpost to 'The Shepherd's Path.' Another mile and its all downhill," Lofty replied, but even as he spoke the van jibbed. A hundred meters further on it spluttered to a standstill. "Now we'll have to push the bloody thing," he finished.

"Why does the road have to go uphill to go down the glen?" Shorty moaned.

"You ken fine it's to skirt the muir. It's nae that steep and it's only a mile afore it's all downhill. So let's start unless you want to go back and ask Maggie to come and gie us a hand," Lofty snapped.

"Watch what you're saying. She might hear you," Shorty replied, staring warily into the murky gloom.

"Bugger Maggie! Stop blethering and get out and shove or we'll be here all night."

Still moaning, Shorty pulled a Balaclava over his head, wrapped his lumber jacket round himself, and joined his brother. Together they heaved against the back of the van and slowly it began to move forward. Each time they reached a corner, or the van veered off track, Shorty dashed to the driver's door and grabbed the steering wheel, at the same time pushing as best he could against the door-pillar. There were no down slopes on that mile of road to give them a respite before the final descent to the village.

The brothers were well out of sight by the time Sandy reached the signpost to 'The Shepherd's Path'. He knew the way as a shortcut used by walkers to bypass the bends and upward gradient of the section of road ahead and decided to take that route. He and Jenny had strolled along it many times, but he forgot that the burn they crossed on the steppingstones would now be in spate. By the time he reached the road again his boots squelched with every step.

He was sitting on a boulder wringing out his socks when the MacLean's van appeared silently out of the mist and stopped by him. Unseen at the back the two brothers leant against the rear doors for a moment to gain breath. They had run out of the energy to argue a long way back.

Anticipating a lift Sandy gathered up his soaking footwear, hobbled to the van, opened the front passenger's door, scrambled in and slammed the door shut.

"Thanks, it's not a night for walking," he said, turning to the driver. But there was no driver.

For a few seconds he was nonplussed; then, as he realised the van was beginning to roll silently forward, he snatched the passenger door handle which, to his horror, came off in his hand. Securing it was one of the many repair jobs that Shorty had been putting off. Frantically, he tried to push it back into place but without success.

Unaware that they now had a passenger, the brothers were putting all the energy they had left into what they hoped would be the final push.

As the road levelled out before it started on its downward gradient Lofty said to Shorty, "We're almost there; you best get by the driver's door ready to jump in when it starts rolling," and even as he spoke the van became easier to push. "Hurry!" he shouted.

Shorty ran forward and grabbed the offside door handle, then saw, through the misted window, a hunched figure with long grey hair in the passenger seat.

"It's her!" he gasped and stepped back.

The van rolled past him with Lofty still pushing. "What the Hell are you doing?" Lofty shouted.

"She's in there!" Shorty shouted back.

"Who's in where?" Lofty asked, stopping pushing for a moment.

"Maggie! In the van! I telt you!"

"Dinna talk daft," Lofty said, and as he spoke the van started to roll forward on its own. He made a grab at the rear door handle but it slipped through his fingers as the door swung open and the van disappeared into the mist.

Inside, Sandy looked up from trying to open the passenger's door and realised that the van was gathering speed. "Stop!" he shouted, but the only response was the clatter of the swinging rear doors. He grabbed the handbrake, a device that the MacLean brother's rarely used so never checked, and applied it. The van continued to gain speed. In desperation he stood up as best he could in the confined space and, using both hands, gave the lever a mighty yank. The van responded to this unusual procedure by swerving violently, sending Sandy sprawling across the seats, and careering off the road where it came to a sudden standstill axle deep in boggy ground.

Sandy heaved himself up onto the passenger seat and looked cautiously round the back of the vehicle. It was completely empty. He decided that the sooner he got out the better so he wound down the nearside window, opened the door from the outside, grabbed his shoes and socks, and stepped out onto the boggy ground.

He squelched his way round the van to the road and was about to sit down and put on his footwear when he heard voices coming out of the mist. The best policy, he decided, would be to conceal himself and await developments. There were gorse bushes on a mound a few metres from the road and he hobbled to them, muttering curses as dead gorse and heather pricked his bare feet, and lay down behind them.

As he waited the shock caught up with him and he started to shiver. He pulled the muffler up to cover the lower half of his face. Its warmth made him feel better and the strong smell of jasmine gave him a reassurance.

It wasn't long before a tall thin figure followed by a short rotund one loomed out of the gloom.

"I tellt you; It was her," the short one was saying.

"It's a pity she couldna drive. There's the van in the bloody bog. How d'you suppose we'll get that out?" the tall one replied.

Shorty stopped abruptly, but Lofty squelched off the road and looked into the van. "Nothing in here," he said.

Shorty approached cautiously. "Nothing! What's that smell of perfume then?" he asked triumphantly.

Lofty put his head into the van, and sniffed deeply. "There's a strong smell there to be sure."

"Apart from your aftershave, where do you suggest it comes from?" Shorty asked.

"Ghosts dinna use scent."

"This one does."

Reassured that he was not in any danger Sandy got to his feet and waved. Standing on the mound, a shadowy figure outlined against the dank grey mist, he looked every bit of eight feet tall.

Shorty saw him first. He grabbed his brother's arm. "Holy Mother, there she is, Maggie herself," he said, crossed himself twice and set off down the hill to the village as fast as he could run.

Lofty turned, and as he did so an eddy of mist swirled round Sandy's head and shoulders like a halo. With a strangled gasp he too was gone, following his panting brother and leaving a bemused Sandy standing, holding his socks and boots.

About the time the Maclean brothers ran out of petrol Red Cameron was in the village bar at the foot of the glen with a bunch of locals that included his cousin Willie Cameron and a few visitors. With Halloween approaching the latter had turned the conversation to Maggie and her alleged appearances.

"I dinna go on the muir much but Red here lives on it and he reckons he's never seen her," Willie said in answer to a query from one of them.

"I havena," Red responded, "but there's plenty that have and more strange things happen on the muir than I care to know about. Only a fool mocks the spirits."

"So you're not worried cycling home on an October night like this?" the questioner asked.

Red shrugged. "I dinna reckon our Maggie would be interested in an old sinner like me, but I'll tell her you'd like to meet her if she comes my way and now I'll be going. I've a heifer due to calf afore long."

For anyone less hardened to life on the Scottish muirs than Red the effect of the dank mist on the amount of alcohol he had consumed might have been disastrous; but he only paused long enough to pull up the hood on his cloak before setting off, a little unsteadily, on his bicycle.

When he reached the outskirts of the village where the road rose more steeply he dismounted and walked, pushing his bicycle on his off side. He was nearing the top of the slope when the MacLean's van came out of the mist. It was at that moment that Sandy stood up and gave the handbrake a mighty yank sending the vehicle swerving across the road straight at Red who jumped off the road with surprising agility.

The van caught the bicycle a glancing blow and Red finished up in the heather with his bicycle on top of him, winded but unharmed. In the van Sandy was too intent on trying to stop the vehicle to see what had just occurred and the sound of hitting the bicycle was drowned by the banging of the van's rear doors.

Red was left with two clear images imprinted in his mind, the Maclean brothers' van coming straight at him and a dark figure with long hair in the passenger's seat.

He lay for some time on the damp ground in a state of shock so didn't see two shadowy figures pass on the other side of the road but heard Shorty's voice coming out of the mist a minute later, calling out, "Holy Mother, there she is, Maggie herself," and the words penetrated his befuddled senses. With a great effort he stood up, carefully examined his bicycle with the gravity of someone slightly drunk and decided it was fit to ride.

Red was sure it was Shorty's voice he had heard and he was almost certain that it had been the Maclean's van that had hit him. He considered the Maclean brothers rather feckless and his shock slowly burnt into anger. He mounted his bicycle and set off in the direction from which the voice had come.

He didn't have to go far before he saw the bogged down van just off the road. A feeling of satisfaction appeased his anger slightly. He dismounted and looked into the van but it was empty. He noticed the smell of perfume and wondered who had been in the van with the brothers and recalled seeing a dark figure with long hair as it headed for him; it certainly hadn't been a Maclean brother. There was no sign of the occupants, and he assumed that they were walking down to the village. He hesitated, confused, not sure what to do.

At that moment, Sandy finished tying his shoelaces and stood up. He had no idea that Red was in the vicinity and started to walk round the gorse bushes towards the van. Red saw him coming out of the mist, a towering grey figure with flowing locks. A light breeze swirled the mist around the apparition and Red smelt the same perfume as he had in the van. He remembered Shorty's words, "Maggie herself," and didn't hesitate any longer but mounted his bicycle and set off as fast as he could back down the hill to the safety of the village. Halfway there he passed the MacLean brothers sitting on a boulder while they regained their breath but he neither saw them nor heard them call out.

Miraculously he reached the bar without falling off his bicycle and burst in. There was complete silence for a few seconds as the drinkers stared in amazement at the dishevelled Red with fragments of heather and moss stuck to his cloak before one of the visitors asked, "Been rolling in the heather with Maggie?"

"Haud your tongue," Willie snapped.

"You're right; it's nae laughing matter. I'll hae a large Bells landlord."

"That you'll not. You'll have a wee nip on the house to steady your nerves. Then, when you've stopped shaking like you've seen a ghost, you can tell us the whole story while you're still half sober."

Red dropped into a chair near the fire and the landlord handed him his scotch which he sank in one gulp before starting. "If it weren't Maggie it was Satan himself tried to kill me and with the Maclean's van, all of eight foot tall it was if an inch and sweet with perfume."

"Maggie's nae eight feet tall, and she dinna use scent," interrupted an old man, who claimed to have met her, but he was silenced by the rest of the company and slowly the whole story unfolded.

"So what's happened to the Maclean brothers?" the landlord asked.

"They weren't in the van when it hit me, nae in the front, and there was no sign of them when I saw it in the ditch," Red said.

"They'll have run onto the muir. They'll be sunk well down in the bog by now," someone said. There was complete silence in the bar as the company took in the significance of the observation which was broken by the sound of footsteps outside and the door being flung open as Shorty and Lofty entered. If anyone had thought on seeing them the whole mystery would be cleared up, they were mistaken. Their story only confirmed and added to what Red had been saying.

"She was after you, Red," the old man who had seen her announced, breaking into a hubbub of speculation.

"What would she want me for? I'd be no catch for the likes of her," Red protested.

"Revenge! Didn't her father treat her like you treat your Jenny? A bonny lass of her age should be wed by now, nae running round a cantankerous old sod like you."

"He's right," Willie said. "I heard you were shouting at that young vet the other day in the village. Your Jenny could do a lot worse."

"She should be courting a local lad, nae an outsider," Red countered.

"A local lad! That she might have been if you hadna scared them all off years ago. You should be thankful that she's taken up with a lad like Sandy. You best watch your temper. If she up and left with him you'd get guy little sympathy in the village."

Lofty stood up to leave and said, "Maggie or no Maggie, our sister's waiting for us so we're off. Come on Shorty, we've a bit to walk yet."

"I'll tow your van out of bog first thing tomorrow. I'd fetch it out the night if it weren't for the breathalyser," the local garage owner said from his perch at the end of the bar.

"Thanks! Even if you offered to do it now, nothing would get me up on the muir again tonight," Lofty answered and left with his brother.

"What about you, Red?" Willie asked. "Fancy cycling back?"

Red didn't answer but just sat staring into the fire.

"Jenny could fetch you," Someone suggested.

"Nae on a night like this," Red retorted.

The garage owner interrupted, "I'll ring round and find someone to drive my taxi. Do you want them to bring Jenny here in case Maggie is still looking for you? I expect Willie here has an extra bed and a couch."

There were a few guffaws which Red ignored but before he could answer the phone in the bar rang and the Landlord answered it. "Hello Jenny! You all right?... Yes he's still here, he had a wee accident with his bike but he's none the worse... I see... no problem... I'll let him know."

"I want to speak to her," Red said.

"She says she's too busy at the moment—the cow's started calving."

Red jumped out of his chair, steadied himself and without a word made for the door. Willie moved faster than he had done for many years and stood between Red and the way out.

"You're nae going to cycle back on the muir tonight. You're nae fit to do so even if Maggie dinna get you."

"But yon heifer's calving early!" Red shouted.

"Calm down," the Landlord said. "She's called the vet out and he'll be a guy site more use than you."

Red turned on the landlord and shouted, "All the more reason for me to go. I canna leave Sandy and her alone all night. What would the village say?"

"About time you let them wed, that's what the village would say. You'd be no use the state you're in and with that temper you'd only cause a scene. You're coming home with me. You've done it before," Willie replied.

A ripple of agreement ran through the company.

"But nae since the missus died," Red protested and looked round the bar for support only to realise that no one was with him. His shoulders hunched and he swayed; suddenly he looked ten years older. Willie took his arm and they left the bar together.

As Willie said later, "Things got sorted that night," and it was a grand wedding that Red Cameron gave his daughter. He even drank a wee toast to the Scented Lady, for luck.

# A MATTER OF GRAVITY

"Who'd have thought that one day I'd be in America sitting on a grassy mountain slope in the moonlight with a beautiful girl, listening to the Great Banzai," Kevin whispered to Little Prairie Flower.

"Life takes many strange turns," his partner for the past year whispered back and moved closer to him.

Apart from being dressed in white robes they could scarcely have been more different; he, a recently reformed, wiry little cat burglar in his mid-thirties, and she, contrary to her sobriquet, a tall willowy woman of twenty-five with fair hair hanging loose to her waist.

The first of the several strange turns of events that led Kevin from his life of crime to his present reformed state occurred two years before, at six o'clock on a fine summer's morning, on the other side of the Atlantic in the Yorkshire Dales. Wearing a 'T' shirt and jeans, Kevin had been walking along a riverbank by meadows still wet with early morning dew some miles away from his suburban home when it all started.

He had stopped for a few minutes with his back to the river to watch the mist silently dispersing from the fields. He found nothing more relaxing after a stressful night's work than the solitude of the Dales in the early morning and on that day he badly needed the soothing environment. Improved security in the larger country houses had made his job much harder and it had been a long time since he had last attempted two break-ins in one night.

He took his state-of-the-art mobile out of his pocket to check on the local radio programme if his nocturnal activities had made the early morning news bulletins. They had, but the police said there was nothing to report at the present stage of their investigations.

He smiled with self-satisfaction and was returning the instrument to his pocket when, without warning, something heavy hit him in the back and sent him sprawling facedown on the grass.

"Oh dear!" a voice boomed above him.

Police! was his first thought, but then he realised that this couldn't be the police. Whoever heard a police officer say "Oh dear?"

The voice boomed again. "Are you alright?" and a pair of patent leather shoes landed on the grass uncomfortably close to his face.

Dazed and winded, Kevin struggled to his feet and found himself staring at a vast expanse of white shirt. Slowly raising his gaze past a black bowtie, he saw that his assailant was male and well over six foot tall. Further scrutiny revealed that he had the build of a rugby forward and was wearing a dinner jacket.

A bouncer on his way home, was Kevin's next thought.

"Sorry! The wind caught me unexpectedly," the man said.

"That wasn't my fault. Probably something you ate," Kevin said, and then thought perhaps he should have kept quiet. A wiry little cat burglar was no match for this giant.

A fleeting smile crossed the man's rugged face, then a look of concern as he said, "Your nose is bleeding."

"What do you expect?" Kevin replied and stepped back to size up the situation. He dismissed the bouncer theory and decided he was not in any immediate danger.

"I should never have done it!" the man said.

"I'd go along with that," Kevin agreed, as he tried to think of a rational explanation as to why this stranger should thump him so hard on the back. The man showed no aggression. Perhaps he had been cycling unsteadily home from a party and gone over the handlebars.

"A good party, was it? Where's your bike?" Kevin asked, making a show of looking around.

It seemed a reasonable question except that there was no track within sight, only a road two hundred meters away on the other side of the river.

"I wasn't riding a bicycle," the man replied.

"Then where did you come from?"

"My car broke down, over there," the man replied, with the wave of a hand in the direction of a black saloon stopped on the distant road.

"And you nipped over to tell me?"

"I've left my mobile on the kitchen table at home and saw you using one. I hoped you would let me use it to call a taxi."

Kevin looked up and down the river. There was no sign of a boat of any description. Only a farm bridge at least five hundred meters downstream. He would have seen the man walking long before he thumped him in the back.

"Nipped across the river?" Kevin asked.

The man looked at the old stone bridge in the distance and then back to Kevin. He was obviously worried. "They'll be most annoyed. I should have used the bridge but you had your back to me and it's a very important seminar. I mustn't be late," he said.

"Never have done what?"

"Jumped."

"Jumped the bleeding river! In a dinner jacket! Try again. That isn't even funny. It must be at least ten meters from bank to bank."

The man took in a deep breath and exhaled slowly. "Oh dear! They definitely won't approve. But you had your back to me so there was no danger of you seeing me do it."

"Oh dear indeed! And I suppose you misjudged your landing," Kevin said, not trying to hide his sarcasm.

"A gust of wind caught me just as I was about to land and...," the man replied, stopping abruptly in mid-sentence, having obviously said more than he should have done.

"Don't tell me, paragliding!" Kevin said caustically.

"No! Well I suppose I'm obliged to tell you. Not paragliding, we call it jumping in case we're overheard but it's really levitating," the man explained.

"Levitating, and what's that? Walking on water?"

"It's a temporary reduction of gravitational force on the body which permits one to float above the ground, and, of course, water."

Kevin looked at the hundred and ten plus kilo body in front of him. "Flitting like a bleeding dragonfly across the ripples I suppose!" he said.

For the first time the man sounded irritated. "You don't realise how serious this is. We're not permitted to levitate in front of the non-initiated. The group won't be at all happy if they find out."

"I wasn't too pleased either," Kevin retorted as he wiped a drop of blood off his nose with the back of his hand and tried to decide if his assailant was a practical joker or mentally unbalanced, and if the latter, whether or not he could outrun him.

"I didn't mean to hit you. I only wanted to borrow your mobile for a minute," the man said and held out a hand which looked more like a dinner plate.

Kevin opened his mouth to protest but decided that a bleeding nose was sufficient damage for one day and passed the instrument to him.

He listened while the man gave detailed directions for the location of his car to a taxi company. Obviously a local man, Kevin decided.

"Thanks, I'll be off then. Remember this meeting never happened," the man said and handed Kevin back his mobile.

"You'll have to run if you want to be back before the taxi arrives," Kevin replied.

The man looked at the bridge downriver, then to his car and said, "You're right; I might as well levitate now you know about it. Would you mind turning your back on me for a couple of minutes? It would be bad enough for me if they found out that I've told you about levitation but it would be a much more serious misdemeanour to prove to you of its existence by letting you witness the act."

Kevin shook his head. "Not again thanks. My back already feels like a sack of potatoes has hit it, and my nose has bled all down the front of my 'T' shirt."

The man hesitated. "Very well then, but you mustn't tell anyone about what you see. Not that they would believe you. The last person who reported a sighting finished up in the psychiatric ward of the local hospital. So I wouldn't mention it if I were you."

With a growing conviction that the man was mentally unbalanced, Kevin watched him walk a short distance back from the river, turn and run, and then leap into the air as he reached the riverbank; but there was no satisfying splash! Instead the man shot out over the river about a meter above water and started to perform a frantic breaststroke, looking like a gigantic black frog suspended by an invisible cord.

He had almost reached mid-river when a stiff breeze came down the dale and wafted him back to the bank he had started from. Kevin, who was standing immobilised by disbelief, moved too late and was knocked over backwards.

"Sorry about that," the man said after he had helped Kevin to his feet and brushed him down.

"Bloody Hell! You really did jump it the first time," was all Kevin could say.

"I suppose it is a bit odd when you're not used to it," the man replied.

"You can say that again!"

Kevin took a couple of backward paces. A horrible thought had occurred to him. "Are you one of those aliens that are supposed to come down in flying saucers and abduct people for experimental purposes?"

"Good grief no! May I introduce myself—I'm Walton, a solicitor by profession. And you are?"

"Kevin. An occasional night worker."

Walton held out his massive hand. "Pleased to meet you," he said, then, noticing his wristwatch, added, "Is that the time! I'll be late for the seminar. I must fly."

Kevin winced, extracted his delicate fingers from the vice-like grip and managed a smile, which was more of a grin and said, "You did a pretty good imitation a few minutes ago. All you needed was wings to flap. How come if you're light enough to float in air you clobbered me so hard?"

"It's the wind, and a matter of the difference between mass and weight, but we're getting technical and I mustn't waste any more time. The problem right now is that I have no motive power so it's no good trying to float over the river against the wind. I'll have to run to the bridge while you try to catch the taxi driver's attention when he or she arrives."

"You could take off your clothes, tie them in a bundle on your head and swim across," Kevin suggested.

"I can't swim!"

Kevin laughed. "There's a turn up for the books! Birdman can't swim!"

Walton stared at him disconcertingly hard and said, "Are you sure *you* can't levitate? Your eyes look the right shade of green. We levitators all have green eyes, you know. If you could it would be easy to for me throw you across the river."

"Quite sure," Kevin said, backing away.

"It would be no problem, but it does take a little practise and I'm not sure that I would like you to try throwing me."

"The feeling is mutual," Kevin said, but even as he spoke the thought of floating over spikes on boundary walls unharmed and CCTV cameras unseen, and drifting over flowerbeds without leaving footprints flashed through his mind and he continued in the same breath, "You said something about my eyes. Now my missus, before she up and left me, used to tell me that I had weird green eyes and they went just like a cat's when I was thinking; said it gave her the willies. I suppose it wouldn't be too terrible being thrown across the river if it would help you. Is there any chance that you could show me how to do this levitating thing?"

Walton snapped, "You don't show people how to do it. You just can or can't do it. You have to have the genes,"

"Are there many with the genes?" Kevin asked.

Walton shook his head and dropped his voice as he replied, "Not since they burnt us as witches and wizards in the Middle Ages. That's when we lost our identity and stopped using our gift."

"Don't tell me you were flying around on broomsticks in the Middle Ages," Kevin said.

"No, of course not, but we had to stop levitating. It's only recently that we have rediscovered the gift, so to speak, and established our Brotherhood. Unfortunately intermarriage has diluted the gene pool and we now have four classifications, Severely Diluted, Diluted, Almost Pure and Pure. We have no Pure Levitators but I am Almost Pure."

"Good for you! Are there many more like you at home?" Kevin asked.

"No, but some members of my family are diluted," Walton replied, missing Kevin's sarcasm and adding, after a momentary pause, "We've found a few thousand with the gift scattered round the northern hemisphere through studying family trees. Occasionally we hear of someone with a strong urge to fly so we check them out."

Kevin remembered the times he had been nearly cornered on a rooftop and remarked, "I've often had a strong desire to fly."

Walton looked at him intently and said, "Now that is interesting, you certainly have an aura. We'll give it a go. Look into my eyes and relax."

It was not customary for Kevin to look people in the eye but reluctantly he slowly raised his gaze from the expanse of white shirt to a pair of pale green eyes that were studying him intently. Immediately he felt the tension in his body slipping away and stood staring for a full two minutes before Walton broke the silence.

"Gravity is for inanimate objects; say the word *float* and you will feel the power that draws you down slipping away," he intoned, then snapped his fingers.

"Float," Kevin repeated.

"What do you feel like now?" Walton asked.

"Like after a few pints," Kevin replied.

Walton took a deep breath and said, "Amazing, I do believe you have something in your genes. Try jumping up and down."

"If you insist," Kevin replied.

Pleased that they were not being observed, Kevin gave a mighty upward leap, much as he had used earlier in the day to scale the boundary wall round an arms dealer's mansion he had visited uninvited. The result was breathtaking. Walton just managed to grab his ankles as he shot up, and pull him down.

"Amazing!" Walton gasped. "That was a close thing; you nearly disappeared into space. You're only the second case of instant awaking that I've met. This should solve our little problem."

He placed a hand on Kevin's shoulder to keep him firmly anchored and fished a handful of twine from his trouser pocket and said, "We always carry some of this to use as an anchor when we're levitating in case of mishaps. Now you're weightless I'm going to tie one end to your belt, then pick you up and throw you across the river. I'll keep hold of the other end so you can pull me across after you've landed."

"You're going to throw me across the river! Not ever! I've had second thoughts," Kevin said.

"It's alright, I'll keep hold of the twine."

"A bit bleeding thin, init?"

"It's strong enough provided one doesn't snatch. When you are firmly on the ground I will make myself weightless and launch myself over the river. All you have to do is pull gently on the twine to keep me moving. Understood?"

"What about all that mass thing that knocked me over?" Kevin asked, looking at the hunk standing in front of him.

"The twine doesn't have to take any weight, only pull a weightless body. As I said, it will be all right so long as you don't snatch."

"I hope the wind knows that!" Kevin said, wetting his finger and holding it up to test the direction and strength.

Walton didn't reply and bent down to grip Kevin's ankles.

"Half a minute!" Kevin shouted. "How do I come down?"

"Ah yes. Of course; your de-levitating word. How about 'terrestrial'? Now look at me."

Kevin looked into Walton's eyes as he intoned, "Your de-levitating word is 'terrestrial'." Then he snapped his fingers and explained, "When I call out that word you will slowly regain your normal weight. Understood?"

"Yes, you shout out 'terrestrial' and I come down."

Walton bent down again, grabbed Kevin by the ankles, swung him round and round like a hammer thrower at an athletic meeting then let him go. Kevin shot out over the river and reached the opposite bank just as the breeze blew up again and wafted him back over the water where he remained looking down at two large trout darting for cover under the bank. He wondered vaguely if he appeared like an enormous heron to them. Then another thought occurred to him. "Don't shout terrestrial yet!" he yelled to Walton.

That was a mistake because on the word terrestrial he slowly descended into the water.

Walton shook his head in disbelief as he watched Kevin swim to the riverbank. "Now that is even more interesting!" he muttered under his breath, "Our Diluted obeyed his own command unintentionally; he must be purer than I realised." Then out aloud he boomed: "Coming over now!" But Kevin wasn't listening. He was too intent on shaking water out of his mobile.

Walton ran, took a short run and launched himself into the air from the riverbank. "Take in the slack!" he roared as he lost momentum. Kevin looked up from his dripping mobile and grabbed the twine but he was too late, it had sagged into the water and caught on a half submerged log. He gave it a hefty yank and it snapped between him and the log.

"A matter of the difference between mass and weight," he muttered as he watched Walton being towed downstream like a grotesque black balloon.

On the road above a taxi driver, oblivious of the drama unfolding across the field below him, sounded his horn. Kevin looked at Walton, decided that he would eventually reach one bank or other, turned and ran up the slope shouting and waving.

"A good party was it?" the driver said, sniffing suspiciously as the dripping Kevin opened the taxi door.

"Nope! It wasn't!" Kevin replied.

"You can't get in dripping water like that. You should have warned me," the driver said.

"I didn't order your taxi. My, er, mate did."

"And where's she? Still swimming?"

"It's a he and he's just landed on the bridge over there," Kevin replied, pointing to a figure standing on the parapet of the farm bridge waving frantically.

"Landed there, did he! From where, mate?"

Kevin realised his slip of the tongue and replied hastily, "He walked there. I swam the river. We were afraid you wouldn't wait and he has... we have, an important engagement."

The taxi driver looked suspiciously at Kevin, sniffed again and said, "Alright then, I'll put the floor mat on the front seat and you can drip onto that, but if your mate's wet, one of you will have to walk; we don't carry ruddy bath towels in our taxis."

Walton wasn't wet. He had managed to keep above parapet level when the log went under the bridge and the twine had snapped.

They dropped Kevin off first and Walton waved away a half-hearted offer to contribute to the fare. It was not until the taxi had disappeared that Kevin realised he had no way of contacting Walton. He didn't even know his surname. The chance of learning how to levitate properly had slipped out of his grasp. It might be possible to locate the taxi and find where the seminar had been held but that would be only the first move, and he might have to answer a lot of awkward questions before he finally found Walton. He shuddered at the thought; he had an antipathy to answering questions. There his venture into the world of the levitationist might have ended if it had not been for something very odd that occurred one evening some weeks later.

He was sprawled on a chaise-longue in his expensively over-furnished living room downing a single malt scotch to calm his nerves after a narrow escape from a security guard. Summer had turned to autumn and business was bad. This was the third time in as many weeks that he had nearly been caught and on each occasion the ability to levitate would have made all the difference. He had tried saying *float* but failed to experience even a slight loss of weight and on one occasion it would have saved him from a nasty fall when a drainpipe came loose.

His confidence was suffering and his income had shrunk badly at a time when he was saving so he could spend three weeks on a Far East cruise. He might even have to sell some of his antique furniture to be able to do so, and that could attract unwanted attention.

He stared absent-mindedly at a dent in the ceiling caused by a champagne cork, a memento of a particularly successful night's work in better times, and his thinking grew confused as he drank rather more scotch than usual until, suddenly, everything became crystal clear. It felt like looking at one of those pictures that go from a meaningless pattern into a three dimensional scene if one concentrates, only all the clarity was in his mind. He would find Walton and insist that he be told all the secrets of levitation in return for his silence on Walton's indiscretions. In his exhilaration at such a simple solution he shouted, "Then I'll float!" and tried to leap off the chaise-longue but instead he shot up to the ceiling adding another dent.

A firm push brought him back down to the carpet with a dull thud but walking was impossible; each pace he took sent him floating up as well as forward. He had just stepped off an occasional table and was drifting towards the ceiling again when he remembered the deactivating word.

"*Terrestrial*," he shouted and sank slowly to the floor where he lay for a few minutes before shouting "Float" again but this time nothing happened.

Puzzled he returned to the chaise-longue, and stared hard at the ceiling blemish as he tried to recall anything in his meeting with Walton that might help him make sense of what was happening. Nothing came to mind so he decided that he would have to visit Walton after all, poured himself another scotch and lay back. After staring absentmindedly at the ceiling for some time he muttered, "Am I drunk or did I float?"—and on the word *float* he felt himself rising off the chaise-longue.

It took him until late into the night to work out that it wasn't the scotch that enabled him to levitate but concentrating on some inanimate object while he cleared his mind of all extraneous thoughts. He spent most of the following day floating round the house like an overgrown Peter Pan.

It was several months after Kevin had reactivated himself that Walton was preparing a lecture on involuntary levitation, a subject that he had become particularly interested in since the river episode. As he prepared his notes he began to have nagging doubts about the condition in which he had left Kevin, not that he really expected him to reactivate himself. Eventually he decided that the best course to take would be to pay Kevin a visit and try to persuade him to be fully deactivated and if that failed suggest he joined the Brotherhood, and risk awkward questions being asked by the Membership Committee. So, on one of his few free evenings, he made his way to Kevin's semi in the suburbs.

When he rang the doorbell Kevin was taking advantage of a moonless night, practicing levitation in his back yard in preparation for an unannounced visit to a millionaire footballer's home a few miles away. He was also taking the opportunity to clean some leaves out of a blocked downspout while at gutter level.

When he heard the bell he descended hurriedly with a hand full of rotten leaves and landed on a flowerbed. By the time he had reached the kitchen the doorbell had rung twice more. Leaving particles of soil along the hall carpet he hurried to the front door and peered through the spy hole to make sure it wasn't the police. Satisfied, he opened the door.

"Remember me? I would appreciate a word in private," Walton said.

Kevin hesitated before replying, "Alright, for a few minutes, but I've got to go out shortly. I work nights."

He didn't plan to leave until after midnight but there were preparations to be made and good planning was of paramount importance in his occupation. He was not a petty thief, as he had told his ex-wife on many occasions.

He led his visitor into the lounge and the first things to catch Walton's eye were two early nineteenth-century mahogany shield-backed Hepplewhite chairs, one each side of the window; then against the wall opposite he noted a fine Victorian credenza with Wedgwood panels.

"You've got some good stuff here; is it you or your wife who's the expert?" Walton asked.

"Me! I do business with various antique dealers and pick up the occasional bargain. My wife and kids hopped it a few years back with a clerk in the Council Offices who never worked late and, before you ask, there isn't anyone else. "

"You're into furniture then?"

"Only as a hobby. I deal in smaller stuff that's easier to handle. Now what was this word in private?"

Walton tore his eyes from the cadenza and said, "It was about levitation. It wasn't until recently I wondered if you might accidentally reactivate yourself. I hope nothing embarrassing has happened."

"Nope! Nothing embarrassing," Kevin replied and moved to lean on the arm of the end of chaise-longue, then stopped when he realised that his hands were still covered with dirt from the gutter.

"Been gardening in the dark?" Walton joked.

"Nope! Cleaning out gutters."

"On a ladder I hope."

"How else?" Kevin replied, but he could see that Walton didn't believe him.

"Flaunting the ability to levitate is considered a serious misdemeanour by the Brotherhood. Using it for criminal purposes unforgivable," Walton said.

"Then you must be in dead trouble," Kevin responded.

"I didn't flaunt it. A miscalculation of wind-speed led to you learning of my ability."

"And passing it on to me."

"Well, that's why I'm here. But firstly let me make it clear that one doesn't pass on the gift of levitation, you either have it or you don't. I only opened your mind to it, so to speak. Now I have come to put matters right in case it does become an embarrassment to you; in fact, to both of us. I propose to deactivate you and then neither of us needs to worry," Walton explained.

"Undo what you've done! Not bleeding likely. It's no embarrassment to me. Might be a lifesaver one day. Now, if you don't mind, I have a job to do."

The word *job* stirred something in Walton's memory and he didn't move.

"Like I said before, I work nights, so if you don't mind," Kevin continued and took Walton's arm, but still Walton didn't move. He had suddenly realised what had been nagging at the back of his mind—Kevin's description of his job when they first met: "an occasional night worker". In all his experience as a solicitor Walton had never before heard someone describe themselves as an occasional night worker; a shift worker, or simply as working nights, yes, but that word *occasional* hadn't sounded right. He wondered why he hadn't realised what was happening before.

For the past few weeks the local papers had been full of reports on daring robberies and attempted robberies in large houses with the most sophisticated alarm systems; break-ins that had the police completely baffled as to how the thief had entered and left the premises. In short, robberies that shrieked out levitation to someone in the know.

Walton took a pace nearer to Kevin so that he towered over him and said, "Not until I have deactivated you."

"Not a hope," Kevin retorted.

Walton gripped Kevin by the shoulder and sat him down on a Victorian nursing chair by the door.

"You have no option!" he snapped.

Kevin reached out and picked up a cordless phone off a nearby wall-table and dialled. "This is six Willow Drive ..." he started but Walton grabbed the phone, switched it off and tossed it onto a chaise-longue.

"I wouldn't get anyone else involved if I were you," he said.

"Those people won't mind. It's the police; they'll be here like a shot. Police don't like being cut off," Kevin replied.

Walton hesitated, then walked into the hall, turned at the front door and said, "If that were the police, which I very much doubt, I'll leave you to explain your call to them if you can. And, if you don't stop abusing your gift, I'll report you to the 'European Brotherhood of Levitationists' and let them deal with you."

"The what?" Kevin asked.

"The 'European Brotherhood'; the very top Levitationists. They can be very nasty. They wouldn't hesitate to send you straight up!"

"What do you mean straight up?"

"Into outer space without a space suit, where you'll explode. It's their normal procedure for serious abusers of the gift, and don't imagine shouting *terrestrial* at the top of your voice will make any difference. If you have a change of heart about being deactivated before the end of next week, and want to contact me, here's my card," Walton replied and dropped his business card on the hall table.

"Bluffing, there's no such Brotherhood," Kevin muttered as Walton let himself out. Then he went into the lounge, picked up the phone and pressed redial.

A Chinese voice answered and Kevin said, "Kevin here. Sorry to cut you off. A number two banquet with fried rice. I'll collect it in half an hour."

Number two banquet was his favourite takeaway but that evening he couldn't enjoy it. Walton had not sounded as if he were making idle threats. The thought of exploding in outer space was still worrying him when he left to do the job he had planned for that night, so much so that, as he floated over the perimeter fence on his way out of the premises he accidentally dropped a silver salver which landed on the head of a security guard knocking him unconscious.

Next day the early editions of the evening papers carried lurid accounts of a daring robbery at a famous footballer's home and the vicious attack on one of the security staff.

Kevin was not surprised to receive a phone call and hear Walton's voice boom out: "This time you've gone too far. Either I de-activate you or I leave the Brotherhood to deal with you as they think fit."

By next day the story of a series of robberies by an invisible burglar who had viciously attacked a security guard had reached the national press. Kevin bought a copy of every daily, locked his doors and windows and sat down to read the reports. He had almost decided that his only sensible course of action was to contact Walton and be de-activated when he noticed a small paragraph in one of the papers warning the general public about a spate of forged twenty pound notes. Counterfeit bank notes, he recalled, were the staple income of his cousin Jake who had a ranch in Colorado.

Jake and his family had lived comfortably for years on forging hundred dollar bills and official documents. In the past they had invited Kevin and his wife to visit them for a prolonged holiday in the 'Little Ole Pad', as Jake called his spread, but Kevin's wife had said that one crook in the house was enough for her. Well, his wife was no longer a problem in that area; he would explain to his cousin that things had got too hot for him in England.

He contacted Jake who said he would be happy for Kevin to come and stay for as long as he wanted but pointed out that a prolonged visit might be difficult to arrange as Kevin's business was hardly of a nature welcomed by the authorities. Also, entering on holiday and overstaying his permitted time was not to be recommended now that taking fingerprints and eye patterns of incoming visitors was routine procedure.

The alternative, Jake suggested, was not to bother the already overloaded authorities but use his, Jake's, contacts to enter as an illegal immigrant. Provided he wasn't caught misbehaving the worst that could happen if he were discovered would be repatriation.

Before he left Kevin wrote a brief note to Walton saying that he was going away and if he didn't return within a year to assume the worst and arrange for his house, furniture and belongings to be given to his children. He asked the Chinese takeaway delivery man to witness his signature and left it on the kitchen table in an envelope addressed, 'A matter of gravity for my Solicitor's attention.'

The 'Little Ole Pad' was in the White River Forest region. To Kevin, when he arrived, it looked like a film set for Dallas with the ranch house, out buildings and corral surrounded by white rail fencing and set in wide open rich green countryside with a distant background of hazy mountains. The only stipulation Jake made was that Kevin mustn't follow his normal occupation while in America; apart from the danger of him being shot it would focus the attention of local law enforcers on the district which might make it difficult for Jake to pursue his business.

As there would be no reason to use his gift of levitation Kevin decided not to mention it. He also had an uneasy feeling that there might be an 'American Brotherhood of Levitationists'. However, this didn't stop him from practising in the woods behind Jake's pad whenever there was no-one about, and a pair of local bald eagles soon came to accept as normal a member of Homo sapiens drifting past them as they roosted.

It was not long before Jake had introduced him to the forgery business and Kevin settled into a lifestyle he had only previously dreamt about. So time slipped by, with Kevin gradually becoming more and more involved in Jake's enterprise, until the night of the raid.

It had been a hot sticky day and the cousins had been working late on the forging press to complete an export order for roubles when it happened. Kevin had taken a shower before retiring and, draped in one of the large white bath-sheets that Jake had imported from England, had gone to the bar and poured himself a Jack Daniels. Suddenly, without warning, the 'Little Ole Pad' was illuminated on all sides.

Kevin froze, one hand holding a glass and the other the bath-sheet in place. An amplified voice shattered the still night. "State Police! We've got you covered. Come out one at a time hands on your head and lie down."

"Hell! Do what they say Kevin, they're sure not playing games," Jake called out from his bedroom and then went to round up his family

Kevin was heading for the front door when he noticed that the side door giving access to the passageway between the homestead and the 'old bunkhouse', in reality the kids' playroom, was still open. The area was in the shadows cast by the now floodlit buildings and it gave him an idea.

His UK operations had taught him that no one looked above roof level for people escaping so he took a chance. He nipped out into the passage, gripped his bath sheet tightly and concentrated on the silhouette of the bunkhouse roof. When he was ready he bent his knees, whispered "Float", gave a mighty upward push and shot vertically into the air.

As he rose above roof level a stiff breeze caught him and he was swept away clinging tightly to his bath sheet. All he had to do now was to find somewhere to land where a naked man with a large bath sheet wrapped round him wouldn't be too out of place, like a midnight skinny dipping party, but that was going to be difficult to find in the dark.

His choice was further limited by the problem of changing direction and he was soon heading out over empty countryside towards the distant mountains that he had often admired from his bedroom window.

In the mountains, unaware of the approaching Kevin, the Great Banzai was standing on a grassy slope in the flickering light of a log fire surrounded by seated members of his Banzai Cult smoking hashish through hookahs.

Despite their name it would be difficult to imagine a less warlike group, but The Great Banzai was acutely aware of an undercurrent of discontent running through the commune. He was a brilliant storyteller and had thought that his stories of The White Robed One would have been adequate to hold his followers, but now they were demanding that they meet this great Guru. Telling them that he was meditating in the Himalayas was no longer satisfying them, particularly Little Prairie Flower. She had become extremely vociferous on the subject that evening and retired early to her wigwam, lacing the flaps securely behind her after telling The Great Banzai that she would return to the Great Outer World next day unless the White Robed One was there in the morning.

Kevin saw the Commune's fire when he was some way off and recalled his cousin telling him of rumours that a strange group of people lived in the mountains. He decided he might not appear too unconventional to them in his present attire and he should make a determined effort to land near to their camp. Overcoming his modesty he took off his bath-sheet and, using it as a sail, he managed to head roughly in the right direction, but judging the landing was tricky.

At what he thought was the right moment he shouted, *"Terrestrial"* and slowly started to descend, frantically wrapping the billowing bath-sheet back round his nakedness. For a minute it appeared as if his timing had been perfect and he would land in open space close to the circle of wigwams housing the commune, but an extra strong gust of wind sent him off course and he collided with the back of Little Prairie Flower's dwelling.

Having been brought up in the Rockies Little Prairie Flower thought a scavenging black bear had blundered into the wigwam. Frantically she unlaced the flaps and rushed out screaming just before the whole structure collapsed.

Still clutching the bath sheet firmly round himself Kevin stood up, looking in the moonlight like an ancient Roman in a white toga, only to collapse in a heap with a yelp of pain. He had sprained his left ankle.

Little Prairie Flower gave a squeal of delight and shouted, "Oh! White Robed One, you have come to us at last!" Then, as Kevin gently felt his damaged ankle, he gasped, "Oh! The White Robed One has damaged his terrestrial self."

For a moment Kevin was nonplussed but he had talked himself out of enough awkward situations to know that silence is rarely the best defence.

Cautiously he heaved himself up with the aid of the tent pole that was sticking out of the tent fabric; then, standing on one leg, he said, with all the dignity he could muster, "A bad landing. A gust of wind caught me. If I could stay the night it would help,"

"The White Robed One can stay as long as he wishes! He mustn't leave before his terrestrial self has healed," Little Prairie Flower replied.

So a very relieved Great Banzai made a wigwam available and Little Prairie Flower became Kevin's self-appointed nurse.

The days slipped quickly by and it didn't take Little Prairie Flower long to realise that Kevin was more terrestrial than celestial. Rather than detract from her growing affection for him it added spice to a mode of living that had become a little boring, although she did make him take a solemn oath not to return to his life of crime; something they agreed to keep secret from the rest of the commune.

It was a month after Kevin's spectacular arrival that Little Prairie Flower said to him, "White Robed One"—she used that sobriquet, even when they were alone together—"I have a feeling that we will have to think up something more exciting than you levitating to meditate in the tree tops for half an hour each day if we wish to hold the commune together. What we need is a colourful ceremony."

"How about everyone dancing round a totem pole while I sit on top of it?" Kevin suggested.

"Too warlike," Little Prairie Flower replied.

"Make it a maypole then; with plenty of coloured ribbons."

"What is a maypole?" Little Prairie Flower asked and Kevin explained. So the ceremony, which they still perform every Saturday evening, was born.

The event starts with the Great Banzai telling a wrapt audience one of his stories. When he finishes Little Prairie Flower stands up and removes her white robe to reveal a colourfully embroidered brassiere, white wrap-round skirt and a deep red artificial ruby in her navel. She skips to the maypole and places a cushion at the base. Kevin, dressed in his white bath sheet, then walks slowly to the pole, sits down on the cushion and concentrates on the artificial ruby to bring him into the state of mind for levitation.

When he is ready he murmurs "*Float*", gives a downward push and floats upward to the top of the pole where he sits while the members of the commune dance round holding the ribbons and weaving them into a pattern that is changed at each full moon.

# TRAVELLING COMPANION

Tom stopped eating his 'All English Breakfast', a speciality of the small provincial Canadian motel where he had spent the night, and stared at the paper. Under the heading 'SCHIZOPHRENIC BRIT FOILS GUN WIELDING PSYCHOPATH,' was a not very flattering photograph of him on elbow crutches limping into the local police station.

Below this an introductory paragraph read, 'Mad 25-year-old schizophrenic Brit, Tom Reason, yesterday rescued a coach load of terrified passengers from a gun crazy psychopath. The only casualty was the coach driver who collapsed with a minor heart attack. Tom, who busted his knee waterskiing on Lake Ontario, dismissed his heroism as a practical joke gone wrong.'

There followed two columns of highly colourful and imaginative journalism which Tom skipped through. As a freelance trouble-shooter on computer programmes Tom travelled widely and filled in time between contracts writing travel articles about the places where he had worked. He reckoned Deadline Dick, his editor, would have sent this effort back by return. On the other hand Deadline would probably have sent back a factual account too with a note saying, 'Leave off the hard stuff Tom until you've finished your articles!'

He put down the paper and continued eating; it helped his concentration. He had to report to the police in an hour to make a statement and his spur of the moment explanation the previous day, that he had thought it was all a practical joke gone over the top, looked even weaker than it did at the time he made it.

A coach was not Tom's favourite mode of travel. He would not have been on one if he hadn't decided to visit Quebec Old City after his injury ruled out further waterskiing.

Driving was out and the very efficient intercity express coach service had the advantage over trains in that Canadian coach terminals are mercifully free of stairs, and fares are cheaper. The main drawback with coaches is that legroom and movement in them is very restricted. As things turned out he caught an overflow coach with seats to spare so parked himself on the aisle side of an unoccupied pair and filled up the window seat with elbow crutches and magazines.

He thought he'd cracked it when the driver shut the door ready to move off, and the window seat was still unoccupied except for his clobber, but he was wrong.

An eye-catching blonde, who had just made it on board before the driver closed the door, was still standing at the front of the coach. She was in her late twenties and wearing a pale lilac blouse under an ice blue two-piece; out of place on the coach, Tom thought, but mighty attractive.

She didn't move when the driver asked her to but looked straight at Tom, smiled and nodded. Then she called out in a clear ringing tone, "Can I have your attention please."

When she was satisfied that she had everyone's attention, she said in a plummy Bostonian accent, "You must remember, I am not really here and never have been. Thank you. Now carry on."

No one made any comment, not even the driver who seemed to have lost interest in her and started the coach on its journey.

The girl walked down the aisle swaying gracefully with the movement of the vehicle as it pulled out of the station. She stopped by Tom and said, "Thank goodness they all speak English; it's dead boring to have to repeat that rigmarole half a dozen times. Do you mind if I join you? I'll sit in the window seat, then there will be no risk of someone sitting on my lap, which can be embarrassing. You can stretch out your leg in the aisle."

"Do people usually sit on your lap?" Tom asked.

The girl gave him a quizzical look but didn't reply. Tom hesitated for a second at the thought of not being able to sprawl across two seats but he didn't get beautiful blue-eyed blondes asking to sit beside him every day.

"Sure, I'll put my arm crutches under the seat," he volunteered and started to heave himself up.

"Better not to move," the girl said with a smile that would have melted an iceberg and eased her way into the window seat, revealing a breathtaking cleavage as she bent over to pick up Tom's crutches and magazines.

She arranged the magazines carefully on her lap, put the elbow crutches on top of them and said, "My name's Gerda."

"Mine's Tom. Are you going far?"

"Quebec. And you?"

"The same," Tom replied, refraining from making a crack about her performance at the front of the coach. He was beginning to look forward to the journey and didn't want to blow it.

"You're British. Can I take it you're on holiday?" she asked.

"Not on holiday, between jobs. I've been working over here on a computer-programming contract. I take it you're from the States."

"That's my home," she said.

"Have you been to England?" he asked.

"Yes, I know England well. I guess you're from Gloucestershire."

"Wrong: Wiltshire."

She smiled her iceberg-melting smile and enthused, "Beautiful villages in Wiltshire, Castle Combe and I just love Lacock, so quintessentially old England."

At that moment the coach stopped to take on two youths equipped for rough terrain walking. Although an express it has pickup points before it leaves the city. As they made their way to the back seat they eyed Gerda appreciatively and she returned their stares unabashed.

"Backpackers!" Tom said disdainfully.

"I bet you were the same at their age," Gerda countered.

"Do you live in the States?" Tom asked, changing the subject abruptly.

"Most of the time. I am going to Québec for a few weeks to reassess the level of smuggling there. It is important to know such things in the laundry shrinking business," she replied.

"Laundry shrinking?" Tom queried but she continued without answering, "The Gallic psyche is so different to that of the Anglo-Saxon. I wonder sometimes if the original French and English genes didn't come from different universes."

Tom was on the point of making a flippant retort but the serious inflection in her voice stifled his remark before it was uttered and his curiosity began to turn into concern. It was becoming obvious to him that there was something more than slightly unusual about his travelling companion, but the worst had yet to come.

Before he could think of a suitable reply she said, "West Country has some very interesting elements, particularly Stonehenge, and of course those hot springs that the Romans made use of in more recent times."

"You think so?" Tom replied. "I've never found the idea of Druids dancing round stones or Romans carrying out their ablutions in warm springs particularly fascinating."

"Oh, but they are. As you know, my ancestors were keeping records of Britain from very early days. Long before those stones were erected. One is able to go back on the inter-galaxy net on *ght.gww.anthology.humans.predruids.som* to your Brits pre-Stonehenge history. As for the hot springs, the Romans weren't the first to enjoy them."

"Is that so? I hadn't given the matter much thought," Tom replied, lost for an intelligent answer.

His concern for the mental stability of his travelling companion was changing from curiosity to alarm. If Gerda had not appeared so calm and amiable, and of course attractive, he might have been seriously worried. He looked around at the passengers nearest to him for moral support, being sure that they must have heard something of his and Gerda's conversation. He was more than a little disconcerted when they quickly averted their gazes as if embarrassed.

When he turned his attention back to Gerda she had closed her eyes but opened them just long enough to say, "I'm receiving dangerous vibrations," before apparently dropping off to sleep.

Tom had never before heard a catnap referred to as receiving dangerous vibrations; recharging the batteries, yes, but not receiving vibrations. He decided then and there that he would take a later coach to Quebec when they changed in Montreal and in the meantime shut his eyes and pretended to be asleep too.

In fact he did nod off. His knee had given him several very disturbed nights, and he didn't wake up until Gerda eased herself past him and walked to the front of the coach where she stood just behind the driver and called out: "Could I have the attention of the two backpackers who boarded the coach after the main terminal?"

That, Tom thought, was hardly necessary; he was willing to bet their eyes had followed every movement of her swaying hips as she walked down the aisle. Having satisfied herself that she had their attention, she said, in her plummy Bostonian, "You must remember, I am not really here and never have been. Thank you. Now carry on."

No one else on the coach took the slightest notice of what was happening, until Tom stood up to let Gerda back into her seat, for which chivalrous act he got a disapproving shake of the head from her and an incredulous look from his fellow travellers. He was about to ask her what it was all about when the coach turned off the road and pulled up at a roadside café for the halfway stop.

"Coming for a cup of coffee?" he asked.

"Good Heavens no," she replied.

"What do you mean, good Heavens no? Does your husband work here or something?"

She laughed, then suddenly looked serious and asked, "You are using telepathy, aren't you?"

"Using what?"

"Damnation!" she gasped, "I should have realised, but it's not always easy to tell; you humans have a habit of moving your lips when you do. Don't you realise that no one can see me? You've been talking to an empty seat. Haven't you recognised what I am? I thought all humans with grade A2 extrasensory perception had been briefed about us."

"What do you mean—extrasensory perception?" Tom asked.

A new thought occurred to him and he started looking around for hidden cameras.

"Of course you have. You're A2. You exude the aura. If you didn't recognise me as an alien why did you let me sit here?"

"That's a daft question!" Tom replied, and she actually blushed.

"What do you think that performance at the front of the coach was about?" she asked.

"Are you trying to tell me that you're invisible?" he queried.

"Nobody's invisible. That's what those performances were about, mass hypnosis."

"But I can see you!"

"Of course you can. You're not subject to mass hypnosis. You're A2, the product of a liaison during an earlier inter-galactic expedition; at least one of your ancestors must have been one of us; sometimes we are almost too human. If you weren't at least A2 you wouldn't be able to hear me. I'm using telepathy."

"Can't I be A1?" Tom asked, entering into the spirit of things. He was certain that he was the victim of a hoax like 'Candid Camera'.

"Don't be frivolous," Gerda replied, but by now the coach was empty and Tom wanted a break.

"I'm off for a coffee. If I can find an invisible one I'll bring it to you," he said and left her.

In the cafe he was cornered by an interesting character heading back to Nova Scotia who had been sitting at the back of the coach, but he couldn't fail to notice that the passengers who had been sitting near to him were eyeing him very apprehensively. When they made a group exit to the restroom he excused himself from the man from Nova Scotia and followed them but, as soon as he appeared, their needs vanished and they left the restroom in a hurry.

A little shaken Tom decided to return to the coach and have it out with Gerda. There he found her reading one of his magazines.

"Must look a bit odd seeing a magazine in midair being read by nobody," he said in what he hoped was a sufficiently sarcastic tone of voice to prod her into explaining what was happening.

"Anything closely associated with me is invisible," she replied.

"What about trying to make me invisible?" he suggested and put an arm round her.

"There's a limit to what can be considered as being associated with me and you're well outside that limit. So let go and don't talk to me anymore unless you use telepathy." She removed his arm, pushing him firmly back into his seat. As she did so a man in jeans and checked shirt tapped Tom on the shoulder.

"Excuse me, is that seat taken?" he asked.

"Yes! Can't you see?" Tom snapped, caught out by the inopportuneness of the timing.

"Now you've really done it!" Gerda said.

Tom turned to apologise to the man but he had already returned to his seat and was muttering to the person sitting next to him.

The bus got underway without further incident and Tom hid his face behind the largest magazine he had, but his brain was racing; he wasn't a travel writer for no good reason. If this lot were trying out a practical joke on him they had chosen the wrong person. He started to think of a suitable heading for an article if these jokers went too far: 'BLONDE PLAYING HUMANOID GOES TOO FAR ON

MONTREAL COACH.' That was too prosaic, he decided; perhaps 'NUTTERS GO NUTS ON MONTREAL COACH' would be better.

He wondered if Deadline would consider a humorous article about a bunch of practical joking nut cases in a coach qualified as travel writing and decided it might be better to try the tabloids.

The article was still developing in his head when Gerda suddenly put down her magazine and said, "Don't answer me unless you speak in a whisper or, like me, you're using telepathy. There, did you get that?"

"Get what?" Tom whispered.

"That telepathic message. Are you sure you didn't hear something? It came over loud and clear!"

"Quite sure and don't tell me you got a telepathic message."

"Of course I did, otherwise I wouldn't say I had. I told you before I was receiving dangerous vibrations; now I know why. It's that man with long dark hair at the front of the coach. He's homicidal. He doesn't know he's transmitting. It can happen when one is very disturbed. If he were one of us he would control it."

"You're telling me you can hear his thoughts!" Tom said. Surely she didn't think he'd fall for that!

"Of course I can; subconscious telepathy."

"You can tell what people are thinking?"

"Definitely not. Only what they transmit. Sometimes under severe strain a person may transmit subconsciously; like that man is now. I would have thought you'd hear it. It's coming through strong enough."

"A sort of silent shout," Tom whispered, intending to sound sarcastic.

"Nicely put," Gerda replied, completely missing the intended irony.

Suddenly she gripped his arm. "The man has a gun and he is going to hijack the coach."

"Oh! Is he?" Tom replied. His article was taking shape rapidly in his head.

A few miles further on as fields gave way to wooded land Gerda grasped his arm again, this time so tightly that it made him wince.

"His wife has left him and he plans to take us hostage until she agrees to come back. This should be interesting," she said.

"Very interesting," Tom replied; she had no idea how interesting. The headlines were getting better by the minute; this was definitely tabloid material.

Gerda let go of his arm. She was obviously concentrating hard. "There's something else worrying him, but I'm not sure what it is. I'll get it in a minute."

Tom was about to say perhaps he's forgotten his lines when the coach screeched to a halt throwing everyone forward in their seats.

By the time the passengers had settled themselves back again the reason for the sudden stop was obvious. The dark haired man was standing facing up the coach and holding a handgun against the driver's head.

"Stay seated and put your hands on the seat in front of you where I can see them or the driver gets it," he said.

Everyone obeyed.

"Just like a bad film," Tom said to Gerda, forgetting to whisper.

"Shut it or I'll shut you up," the gunman retorted.

"Careful! He can hear you," Gerda warned.

The gunman spoke again. "That man in the front seat with the mobile, ring the police. I'll tell you what to say."

"I've got it!" Gerda said.

"What?" Tom whispered, but not quietly enough.

"You won't live to hear what if you don't keep quiet," the gunman snapped.

"Careful, he's unbalanced," Gerda warned, and then went on, "I know what's worrying him; he suspects that his wife has loaded his gun with blanks. She did on a previous occasion before she left him."

"Get her on the telepathic-line and ask her," Tom whispered, more quietly this time, but loud enough to make the woman in the seat across the aisle glare at him.

"This isn't a joke!" Greta snapped so loudly that Tom looked to see if the gunman had heard but he hadn't.

The man with the mobile managed to contact the police and explain the situation but it was obvious that they were not convinced the call was genuine.

The gunman leant forward, grabbed the phone and shouted into it, "You find my wife now or I shoot the passengers one at a time until you do, starting with the fat lady in the front seat."

A buxom woman sitting by the door screamed as the gunman waved the gun in her direction. The police must have heard the scream and decided it was not a hoax call because the gunman continued after a short pause: "How should I know? With her mother; with her sister perhaps; just find her. You tell her to come back."

There was another short pause before he shouted again, "Why do you want to know my name? It's my wife you have to find. Her name is Mari. You find her quick!" Then he turned off the phone and stood looking round the coach.

No one moved; they hardly seemed to be breathing. Tom was amazed how one man with a gun could terrify a coach load of people. He was sure now that only a few of the passengers were in on the hoax. He wondered if any of the others had a gun. If so the joke might have had a tragic ending. Had they been in America, not Canada, somebody might well have been carrying one.

The mobile phone rang. The gunman ignored it but it continued ringing. "Turn it off!" he shouted at the owner who promptly did so.

The situation was becoming less and less like a hoax. Tom looked around at the expressions on the faces of the passengers nearest to him and decided if it were they were certainly not in on it. Something had to be done.

He spoke to the gunman. "That'll be the police wanting more details to help them find your wife. Like your family name," he suggested.

"You say too much. You keep quiet or I shoot you now," the gunman replied.

At that moment the driver gave a strangled gasp and slumped over the wheel. The gunman shook him. Someone in the coach called out, "Get a doctor."

"He only fainted," the gunman said.

"Let me ring for a doctor," the owner of the mobile phone asked.

The gunman was nonplussed and didn't reply.

Tom leaned back in his seat and whispered to Gerda, "If you're invisible why don't you get the gun now his attention has been diverted?"

"I told you. I'm not invisible. If I walk down the aisle he might sense something in his present state of agitation and then he would come out of his trance, see me and shoot me," she replied.

"So you think the gun is loaded after all?" Tom whispered.

"I didn't say definitely it wasn't," Gerda replied.

"If you don't want to walk up the aisle why don't you crawl up and grab him while I hold his attention," Tom suggested. "He's not looking at the floor."

"Are you sure? Right! Here goes," Gerda said and before Tom could protest that it was only a suggestion she had slipped to the floor, pushed his legs to one side and was crawling up the aisle.

Tom winced as a pain from his damaged knee shot up his leg.

The gunman glared at him and shouted, "You stop moving or I shoot."

Gerda stopped crawling and Tom, with a muffled groan, eased himself up a fraction in the seat. "Cramp. I must stand up," he said.

Gerda continued crawling up the aisle and for the first time Tom was convinced no one else could see her.

The gunman said, "You do and I shoot!"

"I can't help it. Haven't you ever had cramp? Anyway you're not a murderer. I bet there are only blanks in that gun."

"I shoot you to prove it," the gunman replied.

"If you did, that would prove nothing to me because I'd be dead and you would never see Mari again because you'd be locked up for the rest of your life." The gunman looked confused and Tom saw that Gerda had almost reached the end of the aisle. "If you want to prove it's loaded, why not shoot out a window," he finished.

"So! I prove it!" the gunman said, aimed at the window and pressed the trigger.

Several things happened in rapid succession. There was a loud bang, the sound of shattering glass, screams from a couple of passengers and a grunt from the gunman as the invisible Gerda grabbed his wrist and head butted him in the face.

Ignoring the pain from the damaged cartilage in his knee, Tom went down the aisle in three hops on his good leg, knocked the gun out of the gunman's hand with one of his elbow crutches and pinned him against the windscreen. The hijack was over but Tom's problems had just started.

Gerda rushed back to her seat in the coach before anyone had time to move into the aisle.

"Well done that man!" someone shouted from the back.

Someone else who had been sitting near him said, "I told you he was bloody mad."

Then a police siren blared outside. Someone opened the coach door and the buxom woman on the front seat scrambled out.

"That woman! Lie down with your hands on your head," an amplified voice shouted and the woman fainted.

The man with the mobile retrieved it from where the gunman had dropped it and contacted the police again. After a few minutes of discussion the amplified voice instructed the gunman to leave the coach with his hands on his head and walk to the police cars. Once he had been dealt with a paramedic came to the coach to attend to the driver and the buxom woman while a police officer instructed everyone else to leave and wait by the roadside.

Tom dismounted first and, as he hobbled clear of the coach he saw Gerda speak to the police officer, then walk off the road into the scrub and disappear from sight.

The dash up the coach hadn't improved Tom's knee which was now almost unbearably painful but the police were far from sympathetic. They wanted to know what made him think the gun was not loaded. He told them that he had thought the whole affair to be a hoax, probably a new TV programme. He considered they were more likely to believe that than an explanation involving an invisible, mind reading blonde travelling companion who had slipped out of the coach and disappeared unnoticed by them. They didn't believe him anyway and their disbelief was enforced by fellow passengers telling them that he had been talking to an empty seat for most of the journey.

"Disarming a psychopath was a matter for specially trained members of the police force, not a schizophrenic crank," was how the interrogating officer put it. He supposed he was lucky to be staying in a hotel overnight and not a psychiatric ward in a local hospital.

He finished his English breakfast—it took a lot to dampen Tom's appetite—paid his bill and limped out onto the sidewalk with his backpack. A cab pulled up alongside him.

The driver leant across, opened the passenger's door and called out, "Want a cab, buddy?"

Tom hobbled to the cab, threw his backpack and elbow crutches onto the back seat and said, "Sure, the main police station, wherever that is."

They had not travelled far when the driver pulled up outside a supermarket.

"You get out here," he instructed, and added: "Gerda wants a word with you before you speak to the cops. Just hobble into the supermarket and she'll catch up with you. I'll be waiting."

At first Tom didn't recognise the raven-haired woman who trundled her shopping trolley laden with groceries towards him, but her eyes and smile gave her away.

"Why the disguise?" Tom asked as he joined her.

"In case someone who shouldn't sees me with you. You're notorious. Haven't you seen the papers? Come with me and pay for this lot like any good husband and we can have a chat in the cab," she said.

"Now what did you tell the police?" Gerda asked as the cab drew away from the kerb.

"Basically that I thought it was all a bad joke. They didn't believe me and I've got to be back in the station in fifteen minutes, by which time I have to have decided whether I stick to my story despite half the passengers thinking I'm mad or tell them the truth in which case everyone *will* think I'm mad."

Gerda laughed. "Decisions, decisions, decisions! Life's full of them but not many as big as the one you have to make now. As you will have noticed, we have contacts, even in this provincial town, and I believe that current thinking of the authorities is to deliver you to the NHS in England as quickly as possible, certainly before the press build you up into some sort of mentally unbalanced hero."

"Hand me over to the NHS! Do you really think they might?"

"Definitely, it's the easy option. They really can't charge you with any crime but the driver and the passenger who fainted might have a case, as the hold up artist was on early release from his previous exploit and you could be called as a witness. That would be embarrassing."

"So what's the alternative?"

"As you are a Grade A2 I've been authorised to make you an offer. You may recall I inadvertently mentioned that I was in the Laundry Shrinking Business."

"Yes, and you ignored me when I asked you what it was."

"Well, it's strictly confidential and a risky game."

"Probably is when the customers get their shrunk shirts back!"

"This is not the time to be facetious. There is a huge amount of money involved. You must know that people are making fortunes in drug dealing but all the money has to be laundered back into circulation. Now, due to in-depth checking of applicants for executive posts, we have problems these days when applying for a job that gives us the opportunity to travel and carry out our research into human behaviour. So a select group of us fund the project with drug money by taking the cash before it is laundered; hence the term 'Laundry shrinking'."

"And the authorities have no idea?"

"Not about us, and we use our hypnotic power whenever we can to remain unseen, hence the performance in the coach. We tip the police off anonymously about the smuggling operation after we have the money; although they must suspect something is wrong when they never find any cash."

"It sounds a dangerous business, even allowing for your ability to fade into the background, so to speak."

"It's not for faint hearts! But no risks, no profit! Unfortunately these days even crooks are using modern security systems and the risks are becoming too great; you can't hypnotise a CCTV camera. On the other hand hacking into illegal overseas bank accounts is becoming increasingly easy and the theft of hot money is rarely reported! Not as stimulating as taking the cash but it does leave more time for relaxation."

"And you think my expertise might be of assistance?" Tom asked rhetorically. The idea of becoming involved in anything at all with Gerda had definite appeal, especially if it included relaxing with her, but there was an immediate problem. "Not that easy from a NHS psychiatric ward!" he added.

Gerda pulled off her raven hair wig, shook out her natural blonde hair and laughed. "But not that difficult from my spread in Brazil; decisions, decisions, decision—I leave it to you!"

# A HORSE ON THE BONNET

As I sat down I caught a glimpse of a silver star almost out of sight down the side of the taxi's seat.

He's been at a wedding, I thought, and wondered if the badly dented bonnet had anything to do with that, perhaps horseplay that escalated out of hand. Dented taxis worry me. If there had been another available I would have taken it.

"The airport," I said.

"A fair way, that. Cost you fifty quid," the driver said.

"Okay by me," I replied, and added, "Nasty dents in the bonnet."

It was a stupid comment I thought, as soon as I had said it. Taxi drivers can be sensitive about anything implying criticism of their driving.

For the first mile he was silent; then he turned his head sideways to speak to me and said, "Hoof marks, those."

"A horse on the bonnet!  Must have been alarming," I replied.

"You could say so. Of course, I haven't told my mates. They think it was the mob in the next town. They can turn rough if they find you in their area."

"Should your mates worry if a horse lands on your bonnet?"  I asked.

"It's not as simple as that, you know. I swore to myself I wouldn't tell anyone, but I've got to get it off my chest, and you're not local— are you?"

"No, never been here before," I assured him. I could tell by the way the back of his neck had turned red that he was embarrassed.

He drove for another mile in silence; then suddenly it all came pouring out:

## THE TAXI DRIVER'S TALE

It wasn't far from here on a bright moonlit night last week—there was this girl waving me down so I pulled into the kerb and said, "Where to, love?"

"The Fairy Oak," she says.

"Never heard of it," I say.

I look at her carefully, what there is of her. She's wearing a white cloak open at the front, and from what I can see she might have come off the top of a Christmas tree. Pretty face, pale complexion, blonde hair, short frilly skirt, and sequins scattered over her dress. All she needs is a bleeding wand.

"You don't mean the Royal Oak, that's for sure," I suggest, when she doesn't reply. They don't like kiss-o-gram girls there. Cause too much trouble. They had a right punch up last time. Had to get the police."

So then she says, "I'm certain he told me the Fairy Oak."

"Sure it wasn't the Fairway Hotel opposite the golf course?" I suggest. "They have a party there most weeks. They don't mind kiss-o-grams—either sex."

"The last place I want to go to is a fairy hotel, party or no party," she tells me.

By now she's got into the back of the taxi, so I say, "Make up your mind love, the Fairway or the Royal Oak?"

She thinks for a few seconds then asks, "Is there a Silver Wood near here?"

"There's Silver Birch Wood," I inform her, and remember an old oak tree there with lovers' names carved all over it. I'm getting the message now.

"Is there an old oak near the gate?" she asks.

"There sure is but I've never heard of it called the Fairy Oak before," I tell her.

"Only lovers call it that," she says.

I turn round to add that I've heard it called a lot of things but nothing as polite as Fairy Oak, and to give her a few choice examples, but she looks so innocent that I don't.

"Is it far?" she asks.

"It's a long way. Cost you fifteen quid," I say, hoping to put her off.

"That's all right," she assures me, so off we go.

After about a mile she asks, "Can you see the Oak from the road?"

"Sure," I reply, and it occurs to me that she might be on a blind date, and wants to give the guy the once over before she gets out. I don't usually get involved with my fares; what they do outside of my taxi is their own business, but I'm getting worried for her safety.

Anyway, before I can start with my Boy Scout act she says, "I would normally be flying in so I could take a good look before landing."

"And that's your parachute on your back?" I reply, entering into the spirit of things. I'd noticed the backpack under her cloak.

"No, those are my wings," she says. "They're all bandaged up. I slipped off a toadstool the other day. Now I can't fly."

"Must have been a big toadstool," I say.

"Not really, I was at my minimum size then. We fairies have a good size range that we can work within, according to what we are doing. At present I'm at my maximum," she tells me, quite serious.

"You a fairy then?" I ask.

"I thought you would have guessed, but I don't suppose you get many fairies in your taxi," she replies.

"Not your kind," I assure her.

"I didn't know there was another lineage in these parts," she replies, still quite serious.

I'm beginning to wonder whether to take her to the wood, or the local nut house. Suppose she gets murdered, I'm thinking, and the fuzz find out who took her to the wood. I'd be suspect number one.

I'm still wrestling with the problem when she squeals, "Oh look! That must be the Oak."

Sure enough it is the Oak. I must have been going a bit faster than I intended. If one quotes a big fare one has got to make the journey seem worthwhile. Anyway I'm relieved to see there's no one there.

I'm just about to sympathise and suggest I take her back when she says, "Go a bit nearer to that gate. We'll wait there until he arrives. They tell me you can get some weird dates on the Internet."

That really worries me so I tell her not to get out until she's had a good dekko; then I switch off the engine and roll down a short slope to the gate. Just as I get there a head appears out of the undergrowth followed by a bare torso. In the moonlight he looks like a hairy edition of one of the Chippendales, if you can remember them, and he's wearing a Stetson.

She squeals, "He's cool! Look, he's expecting me to fly in. See, he's looking up into the sky. I'll creep up behind him and surprise him."

Before I could stop her she jumps out and runs to him.

"Hey! My fare," I shout, and go after her. At that her date turns round and leaps at least one and a half metres into the air. He's starkers, and all horse from the waist down; at least he has a tail, hairy legs, and hooves.

"A satyr!" my fare screams, and belts back to the taxi. I beat her by a short head and we lock the doors quick.

By the time I've started the engine, the creature is jumping about on the bonnet. Its Stetson has fallen off and I can see it has little horns and large ears. Then it starts playing a tune on a fancy tin whistle. I turn my head to look where I'm going as I back up the slope and see that my fare has her hands over her ears. "Quick!" she shouts, "he's trying to seduce me with his pipes."

I put my foot down and shoot onto the road. The creature does a back somersault off the bonnet, but I don't think it's hurt because it lands on its hooves, and in one bound is back in the forest. I don't wait to make sure and set off back to town like the Devil's after me, which I thought he was.

After about a mile my fare says, "You can slow down. He's a creature of the woods. He won't follow us." Then she lapses into silence.

She doesn't speak another word until we reach the outskirts of the town where she asks me to stop.

"You won't tell a soul, will you?" she begs. "If Oberon finds out he'll be livid, but I promise I'll never make a date on the Internet again."

By now I'm ready to believe anything, but a good taxi driver gets his priorities right. "That'll be twenty pounds," I tell her. Well, I had taken her part way back, and had a nasty shock.

She hands me a little silver star.

"Keep the change," she says.

"What's this, bleeding fairy money?" I ask. Then I look again and it's a fifty-pound note.

I know thirty quid is a good tip, but my bonnet's a right mess and I'm upset. You saw what the creature did and I want to know what she proposes doing about it. Now, most fares would say, "What's your insurance for?" or words to that effect, but not her.

"Here are ten stars, that should cover it," she says and drops them onto the back seat. Then she nips out of the offside door, and disappears.

I've got to admit I'm relieved although I can only find nine stars. Still, four hundred and fifty quid is worth having on top of the insurance.

♣

"Most remarkable," I said, and leant back in the seat. There wasn't much else I could say that couldn't be misconstrued.

The driver's red neck returned to its normal grey, and my journey to the airport was completed in silence.

"That'll be fifty quid, and thanks for listening," he said as he pulled up at Departures, and then added, "I suppose you'll be thinking I'm with the fairies now."

I took my wallet out and gave him the fare, and a good tip, "Not at all. The story was worth every penny," I replied.

He didn't see me slip the fifty-pound note into my wallet, and I didn't tell him that the missing star had gone down the side of the seat. After all, who believes in fairies?

# THE GHOST OF CHRISTMAS PRESENT

The be-whiskered Father Christmas from the agency pressed the illuminated brass button. A bell chimed melodiously somewhere in the depths of the house and a minute later Sybil flung open the front door.

Father Christmas held out his hands in a gesture of helplessness.

"Sorry I'm late," he apologised. "Held up on the M6. A bad accident."

Sibyl was not impressed. "You should have allowed for that. They have a bad accident every day on the M6. I'm at my wits end. The children are becoming impossible."

Father Christmas took in her black designer trousers, embroidered cream shirt and immaculate coiffure but refrained from commenting.

"Where's your van?" Sibyl asked.

"Still on the M6."

Have you got your identity card?"

"It's in the van."

Her husband's voice echoed through the parquet-floored hall, "For Heaven's sake hurry up, the kids are going mad."

"Alright Richard! But he hasn't got his identity on him."

"Blow that, just get him moving before these kids pull me and the lounge apart."

Father Christmas nodded his head understandingly. "Children never change. Should I walk through the house shouting Yo! Ho! Ho!?" he suggested.

Sybil laughed cynically. "Don't be absurd. The children would have your beard off in no time. For someone playing Father Christmas you don't know much about present day six to eight year olds, do you?"

"Enough," he replied, and the parting of his whiskers revealed a tolerant smile.

"We'll see," Sybil said, and then she noticed his sack and added, "Why have you got that? I distinctly told the firm you work for that we were buying the presents."

"Just a precaution; in case someone unexpected turns up."

"No one unexpected turns up at our parties. You won't need it. Leave it by the door."

"I'd rather take it with me. I wouldn't be complete without it. Have you labelled all the presents?"

"Of course I have. They're arranged round the grotto. Don't mix them up; we took a lot of trouble finding out what each child wanted."

"Very efficient."

"We do the job properly or not at all. I'll announce each child. We don't throw ordinary Christmas parties."

"Too right!" Richard's voice boomed out, "This one cost a fortune. Now get moving. The grotto's in the conservatory. Go, ho blooming ho, round the side of the house and in through the patio door."

Sibyl indicated the direction and added, "Mrs. Dobson will come in with the first child. Your firm insisted on a chaperone. She's our cleaning lady. She'll be no trouble. We've put a chair for her in a dark corner. Now you'd better hurry."

In the dimly lit conservatory artificial snow covered the floor. A Christmas tree festooned with tinsel, coloured baubles, and twinkling lights faced the lounge door. To one side was a splendid throne, with plush red cushions, set in a white polystyrene grotto, hung with plastic icicles, and lit with concealed blue lights.

Before sitting down Father Christmas carefully read the labels on the presents. He stopped at one large flat parcel and shook his head disapprovingly; otherwise he appeared satisfied.

As he made himself comfortable in the cave Sibyl's voice cut through the festive atmosphere: "Rebecca."

A timid girl in a simple party dress entered the grotto, tightly gripping the hand of a plump, sombrely dressed, middle-aged woman. The woman released her hand and disappeared into the shadows.

The girl stood and stared, awe-struck by the effect of the blue light on a red Father Christmas.

"What a lovely dress. Did your mummy make it?" Father Christmas asked.

Rebecca fiddled with her skirt.

"Come and sit on my knee," he invited.

She shook her head.

He patted a stool at his feet. "Then sit here."

She sat down.

"Would you like a Barbie Doll Magic Castle for Christmas?" he asked.

"Oh yes please," Rebecca responded, her eyes lighting up.

"Can I tell you a little story about a magic castle?" Father Christmas asked, with a twinkle in his eye.

Rebecca smiled. The ice was broken. The story took only a few minutes, but Rebecca listened enthralled.

The rest of the children followed one by one, some timidly, others swaggering because they knew there is no such person as Father Christmas. Yet they all came out smiling happily.

In the lounge Richard said to Sibyl, "I obviously chose the right presents."

"*You* chose! That's a laugh. I had to ring round finding out. You just bought them," Sibyl corrected.

"Whatever, but how does he do it? Not one disappointed face. He's as good as real."

"He's got a challenge coming up. Tony's just gone in. I've never met such an unresponsive kid. I don't know why you had to ask him. I told you I don't want our son mixing with his lot. His parents—well—they're not our type."

"I couldn't very well not invite him as his mother takes our Ryan to school when I have an early seminar."

"Which was his present?"

"A Roboraptor"

"Ah! That dinosaur kit. I wondered at the time who it was for. Quite good enough for him. As soon as he comes out, send our Ryan in. Let's see what our bearded friend's reaction is to being asked for a laptop."

In the Grotto Father Christmas had just finished having a chat with Tony about his consuming interest in dinosaurs and asked, "What would you like for your present?"

"A Roboraptor," Tony replied.

"Wouldn't you prefer a laptop computer so you can visit all the websites on dinosaurs?" Father Christmas enquired.

"Oh yes! But daddy says Father Christmas gives away so many toys he couldn't afford that."

"I think I might make an exception for you," Father Christmas said, and gave Tony the heavy flat parcel.

With a cry of delight Tony rushed into the lounge.

"Look what I've got!" he shouted.

Sybil watched with horror as he tore the wrapping paper off his parcel to reveal the laptop computer Richard had bought for Ryan. Hastily she pushed Ryan into the conservatory.

"That cost 1k! I told you to label everything clearly," Richard barked.

"I did. The stupid man must need glasses—look!" Sybil replied, and picked up the discarded label. On it was written 'TONY'.

"You damned fool!" Richard snapped.

"I didn't make a mistake. He must have swapped the labels."

"He's going to be sorry very soon. Just wait for Ryan to explode," Ryan said.

They waited, but there was no explosion and after a few minutes Ryan walked out of the conservatory with all the assurance of an eight year old who had just joined the adult world.

"What did you get?" his father asked.

"A battery operated hi-tech robot Dinosaur. We had a man-to-man chat. Father Christmas explained, people like us get our big presents on Christmas Day but he thought that I would find the electronics of this challenging."

As Ryan went to show Tony his present Richard glared at Sibyl. "That Yo-ho-ho Father Christmas you booked definitely swapped the labels. This is going to cost me another 1k—no, 1.5k at least. We can't have Tony with the same computer as Ryan."

"But he couldn't have known what was in the parcels," Sibyl protested.

"I don't suppose he cared. He just wanted to have a go at me."

"But why?"

"People do. They're jealous of success."

"Perhaps it's delayed shock from his accident," Sibyl ventured.

"Well, there's another delayed shock coming. I'm going to ring up the firm he works for and make sure he never does this again."

"You can't get him the sack just like that," Sybil called after her husband as he stormed out of the room, but he didn't stop.

"Can't I just!" he shouted back at her as he slammed the door shut.

Ten minutes later he returned looking badly shaken as Sybil emerged from the conservatory. "Where's that Father Christmas?" He demanded.

"He's gone. He said it was us who mixed up the presents. The nerve!" Sybil replied.

"We mixed up the parcels!"

"No, the presents. He said Tony needed the computer more than Ryan."

"You didn't give him the cheque? Did you?" Richard barked.

"Of course not. I was too furious to even think of it."

"Didn't he ask?"

"No!"

"Where did he go?"

"He walked across the lawn and right through my rose bed. The arrogance of the man! Then he disappeared into the darkness."

"You should have chased after him."

"In these shoes?"

"Did he take his sack with him?"

"Yes."

"So what's missing? What's he got in that sack of his?"

"Nothing, as far as I can see. Anyway, Mrs. Dobson was with him all the time and there's not much of value in the conservatory. What did his firm say when you told them to sack him?"

"I didn't get round to telling them. Their phone was permanently engaged. When I eventually got through, and said who I was, they said they were sorry to have let us down."

"Let us down?" Sybil queried.

"Yes, they had just heard that the man they sent to us was killed on the M6 on the way here."

"Oh dear, and he was such a nice man, especially with your Ryan," Mrs. Dobson gasped.

"That wasn't him, if he's dead. Oh! Never mind. There must have been some mistake," Sibyl snapped.

"None, they assured me," Richard replied. "There were two of them in the van. The other man is in intensive care but able to talk."

"He couldn't have been killed. He was here. Do you think he's injured and lying bleeding in the garden?"

"Either that or he's some impostor. How sick can one get? Remember, he didn't have his identity card. You should never have let him in," Richard snapped as he strode out of the conservatory and across the lawn to the rose bed before Sybil could protest.

"You told me he walked through the rose bed," he shouted back to Sibyl.

"Yes, right through the middle."

"Well, there aren't any footprints. No one's walked across this bed. He wasn't on his bloody sleigh by any chance?"

"He definitely walked right through the middle. I watched him. He called back to me as he reached the other side; just before he disappeared."

"What did he say?"

"See you next Christmas, and probably a few more after that."

www.ingramcontent.com/pod-product-compliance
Lightning Source LLC
Chambersburg PA
CBHW031941260626
47157CB00016B/1873